The People in the Mirror
The City Under Seattle

Thea Thomas
&
Blythe Ayne

The People in the Mirror
The City Under Seattle

Thea Thomas
&
Blythe Ayne

The People in the Mirror
Thea Thomas & Blythe Ayne

Emerson & Tilman, Publishers
129 Pendleton Way #55
Washougal, WA 98671

The People in the Mirror

Copyright © Emerson & Tilman
Cover: Nikki's face by Paul Winter
Thea@EmersonandTilman.com
Blythe@BlytheAyne.com

ebook ISBN: 978-1-947151-34-5
Paperback ISBN: 978-1-947151-35-2
Hardback ISBN: 978-1-947151-36-9
Large Print ISBN:978-1-957272-30-6
Audiobook ISBN: 978-1-947151-86-4

[1. YOUNG ADULT FICTION/Paranormal, Occult & Supernatural
2. YOUNG ADULT FICTION/Romance/Contemporary
3. FICTION/Fantasy/Urban] I. Title.
BIC: FM

DEDICATION

To All who Love
Mystery & Romance
&
Seattle's Underground City

Books by Thea Thomas
Contemporary Sweet Romance:
Canyon Road
One Love
Two Weddings
Three Proposals

***Books by Thea Thomas &**
Blythe Ayne*
Young Adult:
The People in the Mirror
Millie in the Mirror
The Angel in the Mirror

Paranormal Romance:
Amethyst Dream
Porcelain Claws

Table of Contents

Chapter 1
Gargoyle Faces

Speered I up into the drizzly sky at the tall, sad, gray front of the apartment building. rising up into a sad, gray sky, and I thought ... I cannot believe I have to call this place home.

An irritating mist-rain-wetness fell into my eyes as I made out gargoyle faces halfway up the building. I looked farther up and saw wet, gray gargoyle bodies at the top of the building—up there in the shifting mists. So a person could tell where the gray building stopped and the gray sky took over, I guessed.

"Isn't it fabulous?" Dad asked, all cheery like he'd built the building himself and was really proud of his work. He moved the umbrella he was sort of holding over Mom and me around some more, shaking more water on us than if there was no umbrella.

"It's ... really something," Mom said.

Good. At least she doesn't think it's "fabulous."

For some reason we continued to stand there, drinking in the view, I guess, Dad still beaming.

"Kind of shades of Rosemary's Baby though—don't you think?" Mom finally ventured.

"Nah!" Dad said, "Not at all! Wait 'til you see the inside, it just doesn't quit."

Oh boy, I thought, more and more of this. "Well, let's go see it then," I said, trying to resign myself to two things: one; I was actually going to have to live in an apartment building that two; came from some old horror movie.

"Good idea," Mom agreed. "Let's go inside, we're getting wet."

"Oh! Sorry!" Dad, all apologetic moved the umbrella around some more, which made sure we were good and wet. "Well, okay," he said behind us. Mom and I had made a beeline for the front door.

At the door stood a "portly" doorman, tall and round, wearing a dark taupe uniform. Yeah. Taupe. That color that just ... isn't really gray, isn't quite brown. He held the door open for us. Felt pretty weird. I can open doors myself, thank you very much.

"Welcome, Mr. Francis!" The doorman said in a reserved jolly way. "This must be your lovely family."

"Right, Homer. My wife, Clarice and my daughter, Dominique, but we usually call her Nikki. Clarice, Nikki, our doorman, Homer."

I couldn't believe it, he actually tipped his hat. No one had ever done that to me. But then, I'd never been introduced to a doorman before.

Once inside, I saw another man in a different sort—but same color—uniform, on the phone, so

Dad didn't introduce us, thank goodness. But I could just feel him memorizing Mom and me as he nodded to Dad.

"Security guard," Dad whispered as we passed him.

Why whisper? I wondered. We weren't doing anything wrong.

We stopped in front of elevator doors that were all shiny silver and brass, with artistic designs on them like Art Deco, which, actually, I like. Okay. So the elevator doors I can live with. Dad pushed the button and one of the elevator doors slid open. Then Dad pushed "7" once we were inside.

"Well ...." I said after the doors slid shut and I gently shook the rain from my hair with my fingertips, "I just wonder what all the paranoia's about."

Mom and Dad turned and looked at me as if I'd just learned to speak, for pity's sake. They both looked completely bemused.

"What do you mean?" Dad finally asked.

"Those men checking us out, seeing if we have a right to be here."

Neither of them said anything as the elevator door slid open. Dad led us down the hall to "717." The carpet in the hall was so thick I felt like I was sinking in it up to my ankles. It had a heavy, scrolly, burgundy and gray Victorian print. Then I noticed the soft gray walls and the ornate, brass wall sconces every few feet that had these little pink bulbs in them. I had to admit, silently, of course, that the whole effect gave the hall a cozy, warm light.

So, all right, nice elevator doors, nice light in the hall. Not much to go on, but better than nothing.

Dad waited until he let us in the apartment before he answered me.

"It's security, Nikki, not paranoia. They're there for our protection."

"Yeah, well," the irritation I felt when the "security guard" checked me out rose up my throat again, "no more casually having a bunch of friends over after school, huh?"

Dad studied me for a moment, a little frown working its way across his forehead like happens when he has to sort out something new. "I hadn't thought about that, sweetheart. But it'll all work out."

I nodded, thinking, I'm sure my friends—of course, I don't have any friends here, so it's completely moot—but, anyway, I'm sure if I *had* any friends, they'd all just love to come into a stuffy place like this.

But I kept my mouth shut. Another thought kept to myself. Dad can't help it he got transferred to Seattle. Just because I'm not happy I don't suppose I have to go out of my way to make him feel miserable.

Anyway, I finally looked around the apartment, and my jaw hit the floor—metaphorically. The place was beautiful! Walls a pale peach, with solid cherry woodwork in the door and window frames—I took shop last semester and had gotten into learning about different types of wood, and knew you didn't see cherry woodwork that often.

Dad had subleased the apartment from a man in his company who'd been sent to England for a year, so the place was completely furnished. All the furniture was big, solid antiques, mostly made of deep rich walnut, with a couple of cherry end tables. I liked it all on sight. Thank goodness the people hadn't gone in for all that spindly Louis-the-Whatsit stuff!

We went from the foyer into a huge living room, where Mom stopped in her tracks. She quietly breathed, "Wow!" An actual baby grand piano took up the entire corner. And it *was* "wow." I knew this made Mom happy. She'd told us both that she was going to get back to her piano playing if Dad dragged her away from teaching third grade for a year. Mom loved those kids.

The baby grand must be the "little surprise" Dad had been hinting and hinting at for the last couple weeks after he came back from Seattle from signing the lease on the apartment. Mom went straight to the piano, sat down and played a couple scales. The sound swelled in fat round notes right to the walls.

"Beautiful quality," she said, "and doesn't even need to be tuned."

We toured the rest of the apartment. Three bedrooms, two with private baths, a kitchen, a little breakfast nook, a formal dining room, and an actual greenhouse room on the corner of the building with two exterior glass walls, full of a riot of all kinds of plants. The whole place was like out of a Victorian movie. I hated to have to admit it, but it was altogether pretty cool.

"Didn't I tell you?" Dad got just more and more proud of himself as Mom "oohed" and "ahhed" at everything, and I even let out a couple of "oohs." It was that impressive. We came back to the living room and settled on facing sofas, covered in a soft, pale green and peach scrolly-patterned velvet.

"This isn't an apartment," I finally said. "It's a house, stuck up in a building. I think it's bigger than our house."

"I told you it was huge," Dad said.

"You said it was a huge *apartment*. I didn't know apartments could be bigger than a house."

"You're not in Laguna Beach anymore."

"Yeah, Dad. I got that part," I shrugged, my depression returning. No. I was not at home. I was not with my friends. I was not going to hang out at the beach today. Or any day soon. I was not going to school on Monday at the school I pretended to hate, but now missed in a mega way. No movies with friends tonight. No shopping tomorrow.

Yes. That old depression climbed right out of that gray sky and poured itself into me.

Chapter II
Movement in the Mirror

But then I pulled myself together somewhat, and tried to be philosophical. I thought, a few days later, about how there was bad and good in most things. This was something my grandmother told me when I was only three or four and I'd accidentally left my treasured picture book she'd given me at the playground—Tootles Favorite, Funny Friends. When we went back to get it, it was gone. I cried so hard I started hiccoughing. That's the first time my grandmother said to me, "There's bad and good in most things."

About a week after that Mom handed me a package and said, "This came for you in the mail." I tore it open and there I held in my hands, *Tootles Favorite, Funny Friends!* I thought at the time it was magic, but now I guess my grandmother got another copy and sent it to me.

Anyway, back to now and about living in this apartment. On the bad side was the security guard, but Homer, the doorman, had gone over to the good side just because he turned out to be such a nice guy. He talks to me like I'm a person, not a kid, which is excellent. On both the good side and the bad side was the new school. Good—only three blocks from home. Bad—after four days, no one has even said "hi" to me. Another bad—the non-stop drizzling sky. I always felt wet. And cold.

Very definitely good—my room. As big as our living room at home, with a gigantic private bathroom the size of my entire bedroom at home.

And, as I'm not entirely heartless and selfish, also on the good side—how much Dad loved his job here, which I know because practically every day he's said, "I love my job here!" and how much Mom loved that baby grand piano. As I made up my "THE APARTMENT AND SEATTLE: GOOD–BAD" lists she was playing Beethoven's Fifth. It floated on the air like sweet whipped butter.

I wished I had something I loved so much I could completely lose myself in it. The only thing I loved like Dad loved his work and Mom loved playing the piano was reading—but that's not a talent, it's a hobby. You couldn't make more of reading than just ... reading. I was reading the "Horror in the Heights" series. The heroine in the pictures on the cover of the books looked exactly like I wished I looked.

I put down the *"Horror in the Heights, #6—Working with Goblins, Pixies and Gnomes"* I was reading and got up to study myself in the mirror inside the walk-in closet. This closet was the other incredibly great part about my room, huge! closet. A room all by itself. It was next to my bathroom, and pretty much the same size as the bathroom, with a gigantous mirror on the back wall, big enough for me to practice ballet in front of it—if I took ballet.

But it was the strangest mirror I'd ever seen, with a dark, smoky quality. I decided it was all dark and smoky because it was so old. Whatever the reason, I loved the way it made me look. Why? Because everyone always says I'm "cute" and I hate being called "cute." There's nothing special about "cute."

But the dark, smoky mirror faded my freckles, and made my pale blue eyes a shade darker, which looked so exotic. Everyone in my family has pale eyes, and it just seemed to me that people with dark eyes came from exciting places. The mirror made my hair a shade darker too. Now, finally, it had a color I could name besides "dishwater blonde." What kind of a color is "dishwater blonde" anyway? Ugh!

Mom and Dad had forbidden me to "put any permanent chemistry" on my hair "for the time being," whatever that meant—because Mom had read some article about how hair color damaged your brain, or something. That didn't mean I didn't fantasize about having hair that was lighter or darker. The mirror clinched it—I'd definitely go darker!

"Enough primping, your highness," I told my reflection. "Time to get at your homework." Since nothing else was going on in my life, I might as well get good grades. Look to the future, Dad always said. Yeah, especially when nothing was happening in the present.

But—and here's where the weird stuff began—just as I turned from the mirror, I saw something move in it.

I turned back to the mirror and peered into it ....

Then I shrieked and jumped. There was a man and a woman in the mirror, talking to each other in a faded light. I could not make out exactly what they looked like, but they were definitely there! I wondered if I could hear what they were saying if Mom's piano playing would only, please!, stop. Which was why Mom hadn't heard me shriek, thank goodness. But before the music stopped, the light in the mirror faded and the people in the mirror disappeared.

I stood there, looking into the mirror, sort of stupefied. I finally left the closet, pulled the closet door shut behind me and moved to stand by one of the long, skinny windows on either side of my four-poster bed. I looked down the seven stories through the gray fog—it was like living in the clouds—and tried to puzzle out an explanation of seeing people in the mirror.

Then I tried to imagine telling Mom what I'd just seen and realized I couldn't. Mom and Dad knew I was unhappy here, living in an apartment, with the new school where no one talked to me, far away from my friends, and, well, everything about being here. It was certain-sure that Mom would cart me off to a shrink before I could finish the sentence, "I'm seeing people in my mirror."

But what if my mind didn't make up those people. What if they were, somehow, there? Whoa—that was scary, too!

I tried to get myself to go look in the mirror again, but I could not screw up the courage. In fact, the thought of going in there every day to get my clothes gave me the willies.

I went to my jewelry box and took out the huge antique emerald dinner ring Grandmother had willed to me, which is what I do whenever I have a problem. And that means, I talk to this ring quite a lot.

Mom and Dad were always telling me I ought to put the ring in the bank safe with their other valuables because I was too young to wear the ring. But I flatly refused.

"What's the point of having something beautiful if you can't ever look at it?" I'd say, and Mom would say, "Beautiful? Dear, it's ostentatious." Then Mom would turn to Dad and say, "She's got more of your Mother in her than just her hands and her nose." And Dad would say nothing, but nod proudly.

I could have passed on having my grammy's silly little pug nose, and I would rather have Mom's slender, long-fingered, piano-playing hands, more than anything. But I was super-pleased to have any part of Grammy's character. And I couldn't imagine parting with her emerald. Before Grammy left forever, I used to tell her the fairy tales that seemed to rise up from the depths of the deep green stone.

When Grammy passed away two years ago, I could not be consoled. In fact, I still missed her so much sometimes, I couldn't think straight. The thing was, Grammy understood me like nobody else—ever. And she always kept every single one of my secrets. Not that I had so many, and not that they were so important. But she honored them just the same.

Like the time my Dad brought me a probably really expensive clown doll from a business trip. I was only seven, and something about that clown face scared me. I didn't want to hurt Dad's feelings, so I told Grammy about how the doll kept me awake, and she made a beautiful tiny little beaded mask that just covered the clown's spooky, too-alive eyes. My Dad thought it was the most wonderful thing his mom had ever done in her life.

"I can't believe you even noticed I gave that doll to Nikki, let alone actually taking the time to make this gorgeous mask," he said. Grammy nodded and said, "it seemed like the only thing he was missing," and winked at me.

Or like the time I had a crush on Jimmy at school when I was nine. One day, for no apparent reason, he came up to me on the playground and slapped me, hard! I was so shocked, but even worse, he broke my heart. When I told Grammy, she said, "people hurt people when they are hurting. Don't let the way he feels touch your heart."

The very next week he came to school with a black eye and a big red welt on his arm. Our teacher, clearly upset, took him to Miss Sharon, our principle. A little while later from where I sat at my desk, I saw a state car pull up to the school. And then, a few minutes after that, two women walked out with Jimmy and got in the state car, and I never saw Jimmy again.

Anyway, Grammy never said, "You need to be different in such and such a way," like my parents always did. And when I couldn't make sense of a problem, I'd take it to Grammy—she'd ask me some questions and I'd suddenly know the answers to my own problems. I always felt better. Plus Grammy had great stories about herself when she was young. She said she was kind of wild "in her day."

So when Grammy very suddenly and unexpectedly dropped of a heart attack, my world stopped making sense. I hadn't realized how often I had conversations in my mind with her that helped me sort things out. I got crazy angry when she died, so Mom took me to a shrink, who saw me exactly twice. He told Mom there was nothing wrong with me, and that I was processing grief in a healthy way.

The therapist let me talk about Grammy as though she was still around, and he told me I could talk with Grammy just like I had before. Because, he pointed out, my grandmother would always be in my heart, and I didn't have to let her go from my heart. It was the opposite of what my mom had been saying, that I had to let Grammy go. So, anyway, from that point I slowly "rejoined the land of the living" as my best friend, Meechie said.

Then in Grammy's will she specifically gave me the emerald ring—along with a bunch of other stuff that had value but didn't mean much to me. With that ring, I felt I had my Grammy again—I didn't have to share her with anyone.

I sat on the edge of my bed looking into the comforting green stone. "I don't know if I'm losing it or what, Grammy, but I really need you ... "you're the only one I can tell ... there are people in the mirror."

* *

Beethoven's Fifth stopped and Mom came to my bedroom door. She paused in the doorway. "Talking to your grandmother again?"

"Yeah."

"I hate to interrupt your meditation, but could you run down to the corner and get some fresh broccoli and milk?"

"Okay." I reverently replaced Grammy's emerald in its little hidey hole in my jewelry box, and followed Mom into the kitchen.

"There's some money." Mom pointed to a twenty on the counter.

"Okay ...."

"And I think you'd better pick up one of those cheesecakes. Dad's bringing someone from work to dinner. He said not to make a fuss, but we have to have something ...."

"Yay! Cheesecake!" I took the money, pulled on what I called my "duck jacket" because it was so waterproof, stepped into my boots, and grabbed an umbrella on my way out the door, then took the elevator down to street level.

"Miss Francis!" Homer tipped his hat when I got to the entrance. "Taking a little jaunt in the rain?"

"Only because I have to."

"Still don't like this weather?" He held the door open.

"Do you?" I stepped out and opened the umbrella, turning to Homer.

He nodded, grinning. "Love it—as long as I'm on the heated side of the door!"

I gave him an I-can-agree-with-that raise of my eyebrows. "I'll be back in ten, or send the rescue squad!" I hurried to the corner grocer where just about everything was twice as expensive as it should be. Except the to-die-for cherry cheesecake. The grocer's wife made it from scratch, and an entire big, fat, round cheesecake cost only ten dollars and fifty cents. I'd already formed quite an attachment to it.

Dad probably invited this guy over tonight just hoping that Mom would get the cheesecake. I grinned at the thought.

"Hi, Mr. Zingas," I called to the short, round-faced, cheerful, store owner.

"Hi, Nikki, I see a cheesecake glint in your eye."

"Am I that transparent? And lesser broccoli and milk glints. I'll be right back." I ran around the tiny store, picked out a couple pounds of broccoli and half-gallon of 2% milk. By the time I got back to the front counter, the cheesecake was wrapped up in pink cellophane with green raffia, pretty as a present.

"Here's a preview of coming attractions." Mr. Zingas cut off a sliver of cheesecake from the one in the showcase, placed it on a bakery tissue and handed it to me.

"Oh yum, thanks." I gave him the twenty dollars, then inhaled the cheesecake. "I needed that! I've had a stressful afternoon."

"Ahh—the roller coaster ride of being a teenager." Mr. Zingas chuckled. He counted out my change, then gave me a serious look. "Anything strange going on at your apartment?"

What kind of a question was that? And what kind of a question was that—right on the heels of seeing people in the mirror? It made my heart race. "Ahm—why do you ask? I mean, what ...."

At that moment a tired looking woman with five small children came in the store, each of the kids taking off in a different direction. Mr. Zingas nodded to the woman. "We'll talk later, Nikki."

"Okay." I gathered my booty and went back out into the drizzle. As I walked back to the apartment building, I wondered what Mr. Zingas was getting at. My imagination ran wild. I'd almost worked up enough courage to quiz Homer about it, but he was talking with a neighbor when I got to the door.

I got off the elevator on the seventh floor and walked down the hall to the apartment in a preoccupied daze, when I almost literally ran into the most gorgeous boy I'd ever seen in real life. Although he looked at me so steadily as he passed me, I thought I'd stop breathing, he seemed, too, to be in his own state of preoccupation. Neither of us even said "hi" as we passed each other.

I fumbled with my keys and finally got the right one in the keyhole just as I heard the elevator chime and its doors slide open. I went inside, closed the door and leaned against it.

I felt like I'd swallowed the entire cheesecake—

like some giant sweet sensation welled up inside me. I realized that he even smelled wonderful, as the scent of his cologne or soap lingered on. I put the groceries on the floor and stepped out into the hall, following the faint scent further up the hall to the next apartment.

Was it possible this gorgeous young man was my neighbor? Hmmmm ... maybe this apartment living had its up side. I never knew when I might encounter him in the hall, That wasn't even a possibility in a house!

I went back to my apartment just as Mom stepped out.

"Whatever are you doing? I heard the door open then close. Here's the cheesecake, no Nikki."

"I ... I ... was curious to look down the hall. I've never, you know, gone past our door, and I was just—curious."

"Weird, Nikki," Mom said. She was right.

I shrugged. "I have an inquiring mind, and inquiring minds want to know."

"Do you suppose you and your inquiring mind could help me fix dinner?"

"We'd love to."

I was grateful we had company that night. The three adults had a lot to talk about, which suited me just fine, because I could finally think about the incredible boy. Why hadn't I seen him before? Why hadn't I seen him at school? Even if there were a million guys, I'd notice him! He came straight from my dreams. Thin, almost too thin for some girls maybe, but I liked thin guys. Black wavy hair, and dark eyes. Big, penetrating, dark, sensual eyes.

But there was something else in his eyes—and I realized now that that was what I'd wanted to have a moment to stop and think about. What was that other thing in his eyes?

"Do you like it here, Dominique?" Dad's coworker asked me.

I tried to remember his name, but it had made absolutely no stop on its way in one ear and out the other.

"Oh, I, ah ...."

"I don't think she's crazy about the weather, she's a child of the sun," Mom answered for me.

"I can sympathize with that. I came here from Kansas two years ago, and I'm still trying to get used to it."

"Well, it's not all bad," I said.

"*REALLY?*" Mom and Dad exclaimed together.

"Really." I munched my broccoli.

"Young people! They adjust so fast," Mom said.

Yeah, I thought, especially when the 'young person' has an interesting neighbor with mysterious, sad, dark eyes.

That was it! There was a sadness in his eyes, as if he'd been carrying it around—the sadness—for a long, long time.

".... even the mirrors are antique." Mom's words broke into my thoughts.

The mirror! I'd completely forgotten about the people in the mirror. Who were they? *What* were they? Were they ghosts? Or weird phenomena of some sort that could be explained rationally? Were they beings from another dimension? Like Mom just said, all of the mirrors in the place were antique. What kind of experiences, in so many years, might a mirror go through?

"Arg!" I exclaimed. I jumped up from the table and ran into my bedroom and then the closet. The thought just hit me that the people in the mirror saw me in my closet where I dressed! But when I got in there, I realized that I dressed in a little cubby in the closet, at an angle that was out of line of sight for the people in the mirror. Just in case they could see me.

And then I thought, if they were ghosts, they maybe couldn't see me anyway.

"Are you all right?" Mom stood in the closet doorway with a worried expression.

"Oh! Yeah. Jeez, I'm sorry. I just had to check on something."

"Check on something?" Mom's face went from bemused to worried. "Check on what?"

"Well, the mirror. You were talking about the mirrors being antique and I wanted to check mine out again. 'Cause I was thinking the other day, that there was something kinda funny looking about the mirror, and the idea of it being antique makes good sense, now that you mention it. Do you think it is, really?" I was fully aware of babbling.

Mom's worried look deepened. She reached out and felt my forehead. "You must be coming down with something, you've been acting awfully strange today."

"I'm okay—like you'd say, don't be such a worry wart. Let's go back to dinner."

We walked down the hall to the dining room. "I wonder if ghosts can see the present," I mused.

"There are no such things as ghosts," Mom said in a matter-of-fact voice.

"But have they been empirically disproven?"

"That's a question for your father, Nikki. But, please, not tonight."

"Okay, Mom. Not tonight. Tonight we're all cheesecake and chatter."

Chapter III
The Hall of the Mountain King

The next day when I got home from school, Mom stopped playing the piano the minute I came through the door. She didn't usually do that, she usually hammered on, smiling and holding her cheek out to be kissed. So I knew something was up when she left off right in the midst of the climatic frenzy of The Hall of the Mountain King, and sat, poised, ready to say something, as I walked into the room.

"Da-da-da-da, da, da, da! Da-da-da, *DA-DA-DA!*" I sang the next couple of bars. I was in a good mood. One look at Mom's face, though, and I knew I soon would not be in as good a mood.

She pointed to the coffee table. "There's the note about your appointment with Dr. Carcionne. She comes highly recommended and we're very fortunate that she had a cancellation tomorrow afternoon."

"We?" The smile fell off my face. "I guess Dr. Carcionne is a shrink."

"Family therapist specializing in teenagers."

"When will people give up and realize that there is no cure for the dreaded teenage disease? Except growing out of it. Or not make it through it." I slumped onto the couch. Great, someone new poking at my mind, when I just wanted my mind to myself.

"And it's precisely that morbid sort of talk I want the doctor to address. Among other things."

"You're mad at me."

Mom came over, sat on the sofa and put her arm around me. "Of course not, Nikki. I'm worried about you. And I'm not trained to fix you."

"But, Mom, I'm not broken. And besides, you're a great advice giver and ... stuff."

"Thanks, Nikki, but you're still going to see Dr. Carcionne. You'll feel better after you do."

"Which, when averaged with how lousy I feel before I go, comes out to about the same thing as not going at all, except not going doesn't cost anything. Even if she does make me feel 'better adjusted.' Eugh-ick. Don't forget Dr. Jean, Mom."

"Let's not bring him up. That's in the past. He was a sick man, which is why I worked so hard all day to find a highly reputable woman."

"Ignoring the past is not growth, Mom. And ignoring the fact that I had to have a year of therapy just because of a shrink doesn't seem ...."

"Enough arguing, Nikki. You're going to see Dr. Carcionne, at least once. Our insurance covers it eighty percent."

"Whoopee!" I went to my room and closed the door. Mom seemed so different from who she used to be. I threw my books on the bed. Maybe it *is* me. Then I threw myself on the bed. Maybe I'm just all kinds of a misfit.

I remembered when Mom and I had sort of grown apart. I was eleven. It was a really rough time. First, that awful Dr. Jean, then Dad had been sent to England for three months and Mom lost the baby who was to be my longed-for little brother. That's the first time Mom decided I had to be in therapy, even though a couple therapists dismissed me after one or two visits, just like the kind therapist who let me have my Grammy back, in my mind. I had learned enough, though, from the shrinking sessions to wonder if Mom wasn't "projecting" her problems onto me.

I saw my closet door standing open. Mom must have been putting away clean clothes. I could see the mirror from where I'd flung myself on the bed, and, even across the bedroom and through the closet, I was certain I saw movement. Sort of scared, but also, wanting to solve the mystery, I got up and flipped on the closet light. Nothing. Just my own reflection.

I felt irritated. In fact, everything seemed pretty gritty-annoying. Another shrink. Just completely ick. I wasn't adjusted to the apartment or school, or anything, I didn't want to have to adjust to having my interior self poked at, too.

In addition, and what was particularly irritating, I hadn't ever seen the gorgeous boy again since the first time. But, quite frankly, the last straw was this creepy-weird something about my mirror.

I went to the hall linen closet, pulled out a dark blue sheet, brought it back into my room and hung it over the mirror.

I stepped back and looked at it. Okay. The mirror was covered. Contemplating the sheet over the mirror I thought, you know Nikki, there really is something not-quite-right with you. It's weird to put a sheet over a mirror.

So I decided that maybe this new shrink could be helpful, if she'd just not be too nosy. If I didn't want to talk about something, I wouldn't. I had no intention of giving up my very private stuff to just any old body.

* *

The next day, Mom insisted on taking me to Dr. Carcionne's office, when I could have, and would have preferred to, take the bus. It wasn't that far from school, and I was not nine years old. I carried on this argument in my head as Mom drove me to the appointment. It went something like: I'm fifteen. I can certainly take a bus to an appointment. In some cultures I'd be married and have a kid by now.

Well, I didn't want to be married with a kid. But I did feel I'd be okay without the humiliation of my mother picking me up after school and hauling me off to a shrink. However, when we got there—with hardly a word between us the whole way—she at least had the decency to stay in the waiting room.

When Dr. Carcionne's personal assistant ushered me into the "inner sanctum" I sat in a straight-backed chair. I avoided the two beautiful and comfortable-looking wing-back chairs, thinking my chair choice would give a clear message that I did not want to be here.

Dr. Carcionne sat across from me, a plain, trim woman, with black hair pulled back in a tight knot, big glasses, almost no make-up, and wearing a plain brown suit.

"Hi, Dominique," she said. I could feel her studying me as I studied her office.

"Nikki, please." No sandbox—good. No little kids books, no puppets, good, good. In fact, the office wasn't bad at all. Some books, some really interesting art, pale brick-colored walls, an interesting flower arrangement with big orangeish, exotic-looking flowers that I didn't know what they were.

So! It looked like an office for adults, not a kid's therapist's office. All good.

"Your mother gave me a list of your previous therapists—I got a couple of faxes today from Dr. Smith and Dr. Candy."

I giggled.

"What's funny?"

"Oh, Dr. Candy. Mom thought that with a name like that he'd be a good child psychologist, but he was so lousy. He didn't have the least clue how people work. In fact, he quit being a therapist while I was seeing him."

"Because of you?"

I thought she was making a joke and expected to see her crack a smile. But she didn't.

"No," I answered, realizing the session had started, and even if she hadn't put pen to paper, she was already taking mental notes—"delusions of grandeur." "Not because of me. That would be weird. It was, like I said, he didn't know how people worked, and I guess he finally realized it. Then I got Dr. Smith. I suppose Dr. Smith had the ex-Dr. Candy's records, since they were in the same office."

"Um-hum," Dr. Carcionne said, studying the file she'd started on me. "Your mother mentioned you've not been happy with the move to Seattle."

"I'm adjusting."

"And that you've been talking about ghosts."

"Hypothetically."

"Hypothetically. What are your hypothetical thoughts about ghosts?"

"I don't know. All I said to Mom is that they haven't been empirically disproved. Next thing I know, I'm being hauled into your office." I had just decided I didn't like Dr. Carcionne and I was not about to get into anything private with her.

She put down the file and gave me her undivided attention. "I feel we're not off to a good start."

I didn't say anything.

"I thought talking about your discussion of ghosts with your mother and seeing if there's an objective reason for you to bring up that subject with her might be a good jumping off point. I'm kind of wondering now, though, if bringing up ghosts with your mother wasn't a bid for attention."

"I don't need to 'bid' for my mother's attention." I turned and looked out the window. I saw trees and had the thought that that's one thing you missed when you lived on the seventh floor. You didn't look out the window and see trees unless you went over to the window and looked down on them. Or like, if there was an apartment building in the redwood forest I could live on the seventh floor and see trees out the window.

"I'm an only child, I get all her attention. If I can 'place a bid,' I'd like to bid for less attention.

Sometimes I think she drags me to people like you because something's bothering her." There. I said it. I didn't know if it made me feel better, but it was my truth.

Dr. Carcionne nodded. She picked up the file and started writing again.

"Well," I said, "now we're getting somewhere!" But in fact, the rest of the hour went from boring, to more boring, to dreadful.

That night at the dinner table there was an endless discussion between Mom and Dad about "Nikki's condition." Finally, I could stand it no longer.

"You know, I'm sitting right here. I'm not, like a chair or something. And I'm not nine or ten anymore, either. I mean, it hurts my feelings to have you talk about me like, 'oh, the cauliflower tastes a little off tonight,' or something."

Dad looked at me with apology in his eyes. "I'm sorry, Nikki. You're absolutely right. Absolutely. Go to your room so we can talk about you behind your back."

My mouth fell open, then I saw the twinkle in his eye. He leaned over and patted my hand. "Just teasing, Pumpkin Patch. She's right, Clarice, she's not a little kid anymore."

"Well, I'm sorry, too," Mom said. "But I don't know what to say to her when she's accused me of projecting. I was so embarrassed."

I involuntarily shuddered at the memory of Mom coming into the last half of the session when Dr. Carcionne brought up the possibility that Mom was putting her worries onto me so she wouldn't have to face them herself. I got angry and felt betrayed when Dr. Carcionne stated my observation directly to Mom. And then I felt bad to see Mom so embarrassed. Even if Mom's reaction did seem to prove my point.

"Look," I said, "I don't like Dr. C. and she doesn't like me. You're wasting your money, or the company's money, or somebody's money. Excuse me, please."

I gathered my dishes, took them into the kitchen, rinsed them and stuck them in the dishwasher. I could hear Dad telling Mom that she was over-reacting. Then Mom really over-reacted by telling Dad he wasn't around enough to know what was going on. Silence fell between them, and they didn't even say good-night to me when I went to my room.

I closed my door quietly. Some part of me wanted to fling down on the bed and cry until I had no more tears, but some other part of me said that would be a waste of energy.

"This whole thing got started because of that stupid mirror! It's enough, already. I don't believe in ghosts and I don't believe in the people in the mirror."

I went into the closet and whipped the sheet off the mirror.

Well, I thought, it was a good night for arguing. Because there in the smoky mirror a man and a woman were facing one another, fury in their faces.

Chapter IV
Almost the Best Day Ever

Between a rock and a hard place—that's how I felt last night when I'd seen the people in the mirror again. Mom and Dad arguing about me at the dining table, and the woman and the man in the mirror, stomping off in different directions right after I unveiled them so I couldn't show my folks the reason for my weirdness.

I could only cover the mirror up again and close the door to the closet. Then I'd spent a lousy night of not being able to sleep. When I woke up in the morning I was not relishing encountering the stony silence between Mom and Dad. I stayed in my room until the last minute.

"Hey, sleepyhead, come on—it's getting late!" Dad called cheerily. Well, maybe that was a good sign, at least Dad seemed happy. Sometimes, though, it just meant Dad was over it and Mom wasn't. In which case, his good mood irritated her all the more.

"Coming!" I gathered my backpack and shoulder bag and hurried to the breakfast nook. Mom wasn't up yet.

"Good morning, Twinkle Toes," Dad said. "Sit down, I've got something to say. Your mom made a good point that I don't spend enough time with the two of you lately. Well, before we moved I was all preoccupied with getting moved, and since we moved I've had to put in extra hours at the new job to get up to speed. I had it in my mind that in six months I'd have more time for my family."

He ran his fingers through his hair which made it stand even more every-which-way. "But your mother made me realize that's too far off. As usual, she's one-hundred percent right."

"As usual," I interjected, perhaps a bit sarcastically—sarcasm lost on Dad.

"Anyway, I need to spend uninterrupted quality time with the two of you soon. So—I'm taking Friday off next week. One of the guys at work was talking about a fabulous lodge at the beach that he goes to when he needs some time away from it all. I'm reserving a couple rooms for three days. We're going to have some family fun, or know the reason why!"

Mom walked into the kitchen, a big smile on her face.

"Wonderful," I said loving the idea. "Maybe there'll be sun!"

Dad's face wrinkled up into a bit of frown. "From what I've heard I wouldn't count on that.

But it's still beautiful—giant trees, peace and quiet, nature all around, and right on the ocean. Different flora and fauna than you're used to. It'll be fun to explore. 'Totally awe-inspiring,' Ned said." Dad looked over at Mom until she met his gaze. "And romantic, totally romantic."

"I don't mind that," Mom answered, returning her attention to dishwashing.

Oh, great, I thought. Nikki, the third wheel.

My mind got caught up in a fantasy that included the gorgeous and mysterious boy next door. I allowed myself a moment of wild internal story-telling wherein I invited him to go with us. Yeah, right. Like I'd have the courage to do that. I wouldn't, but dreaming doesn't hurt anyone, I retorted to that negative piece of my mind.

Dad put his hand to his mouth as if he was holding a microphone. "We have a blip on our radar screen—it just came out of the ozone. Looks like a UFO—no ... yes ... no. It's—why its Nikki, returning to planet earth!"

"Right. Funny, Dad. I'm right here."

"Tell us, Miss Francis, what's it like out there?"

Mom giggled.

I shook my head. "I'm just thinking about your plan. I can hope there'll be sunshine, can't I?"

"Sure," Dad said. "Hope is great. But don't plan."

At school, my attention was torn between the work at hand, thinking about next weekend, and last, but absolutely not least, keeping my eye out for the boy next door. Yes. It had become my one particular obsession.

Every time I saw a thin, dark-haired boy, I'd oh-so-casually hurry up to him, then slowly, and even more casually, wander by, giving a sidelong glance. But it was never "*HIM*."

I noticed something, though—now that I looked at people, people looked back, smiling, and some actually said "hi." It was pretty amazing. I felt a lot better about myself and school by the time I got home.

When I came through the door, Mom was just finishing something Mozart at the piano. She turned and smiled at me. "How was your day?"

"Good, Mom. Just—sort of the best day I've had since I got here."

"Oh? How so?"

"I don't know why, but a bunch of people said 'hi' to me. Just like that, for no reason."

"You mean, no one's said hi to you since you started school here?"

"Well, yeah, Mom, I told you, no one talks to me. Saying 'hi' is like—talking."

"I thought you were exaggerating. Like when you say we 'never have cheesecake,' but we do, frequently."

"Okay. Let me clarify. Literally no one has talked to me at school until today. But figuratively we never have cheesecake."

"What did you do today that was different?" She patted the piano bench and I sat by her.

"Why does it have to be me?"

"Because if a whole bunch of people spontaneously behave in a different way, there must be something in common. As you are the constant in this situation, you must have done something different. I'll bet the idea of going away for the weekend cheered you up, and you pulled your eyeballs up out of your shoelaces and made some eye contact."

How does she do that?

"And here's something else to make this the best day ever," she continued. "Since we're going away next Friday and have a lot to do Thursday evening, I cancelled your appointment with Dr. Carcionne next week."

I grinned with every smile muscle in my face. "Fantastic! If you'd told me that before I went to school this morning, I would have had everyone in three grades saying hi to me!"

*   *

The next week I was the happiest I've been since we moved to this off-world place. I even began to notice the beauty of Seattle. Okay. Truth, it *is* beautiful. A person just has to get into its mood, which is a very different kind of mood from Laguna Beach.

And, big plus, although I never saw "the" boy at school, I did see him once, going into our building when I was a block away. So—at least I knew he was real. And what's more, it confirmed that he lived there or had some reason to occasionally be there.

Then a couple of girls asked me if I wanted to go to a movie Friday night. I was sorry to have to say I was going to the beach, but when I told them where I was going, they let me know that that was pretty cool. Suzanne said, "That lodge is my favorite place on the planet."

Even more to look forward to!

And then Suzanne said, "okay, we'll go to a movie next week." So it came out better and better, because for the first time in ages, in eons, I had two weekends in a row with something to look forward to.

And poof! It was Friday morning. Dad banged around in the kitchen making breakfast, singing "Someone's in the kitchen with Dinah," at the absolute tip-top of his voice. I crawled out of bed and toward the kitchen—after all, it was only five-thirty a.m. and this was supposed to be a vacation day. I met Mom stumbling sleepily toward the kitchen too.

"Sweetheart!" Mom tried to get Dad's attention. "*DEAREST!* We live in an apartment, not on an acreage. The neighbors will be dialing 911 pretty soon if you don't tone it down."

Dad nodded and turned it down a few decibels, but his voice still surely penetrated nearby walls and I hoped with all my heart that my gorgeous neighbor wouldn't think my dad too weird.

"Dad, it's supposed to be a day off," I pointed out as he—at last!—lapsed into a hummed version of "Dinah."

"Why are you making breakfast in the middle of the night?"

"'Cause, Sugar Lump, I don't want to waste a moment. Get dressed, come have breakfast. You can sleep in the car, if you can sleep while riding through some of the most beautiful country on the little planet known as Earth."

"We won't be able to see 'the most beautiful country on the planet' in the night. In case you haven't noticed, we're at the north pole—it doesn't get light here until noon—or June."

"It does seem that way," Mom laughed. "But your dad is right, it's good to get going early. I'm sure there'll be enough light to see the outlines of trees by the time we get on the road."

A couple hours later, we were nearly out of the city. I realized I was glad we got an early start. I watched the beautiful landscape, the trees, the rising sun, the glint of water, the charming little houses flow by the car window, all of it like reflections in a river. But somehow, somewhere along the road, I actually did fall into a deep sleep and dreamed of the landscape. Suddenly Dad shook me awake. "We're here, Sleeping Beauty, wake up."

"Did I fall asleep?" I asked, amazed.

"That, or an excellent imitation."

I sat up and looked out the window—I couldn't believe my eyes! The most beautiful, romantic and huge lodge lay stretched before me among towering evergreens. A spicy pine-like aroma mingled with a salty sea smell, came right into the car and really woke me up.

I climbed, yawning, out of the car, and my yawn turned to a gasp. The ocean was immediately behind me, the parking lot on a precipice high above it.

"*Wow-oh-wow*," I whispered. "Am I still sleeping?"

"Breathtaking, isn't it," Mom said, handing me a piece of luggage. "As usual, your Dad was right."

"More right than even I knew." Dad dug out the rest of the luggage from the trunk. "It's fabulous. Let's go!" Not even waiting to see if we were with him, he headed for the fairytale lodge.

"Yeah, let's go!" I scurried after him.

We were soon checked into a rustic, open-beamed suite—two bedrooms with a living room between. The furniture, the walls—everything—warm earth and orange and rose tones, with large, rustic, lodge-style pine and cedar log furniture. I stepped out on our living room deck to absorb a breath-taking view of the ocean through the craggy forest. I breathed in the view, the pine scent, and the crisp ocean air. Mom and Dad came out of their room and joined me.

"Incredible," I said quietly.

"Umm-hum ..." Dad inhaled deeply too.

"Starving!" I exclaimed.

"Already?" Mom asked, while at the same moment Dad said, "yeah, me too!"

"I'm out-numbered," Mom moaned.

We ambled down to the dining room. It was built over the rocky precipice and we literally hung out over the water.

"*Fantastic!*" I pulled my chair right up to the floor-length window.

"I agree," Mom leaned back in her chair and looked away from the view.

"What's the matter, my pet?"Dad asked.

"Vertigo."

"Maybe you should sit over here, with your back to the view," I suggested to Mom.

"No way—you know the old saying, 'never turn your back on the ocean.'"

"I didn't know you were spooky about heights, Mom, I thought you weren't afraid of anything."

"A waitress came up to us. "Have you folks decided what you'd like?"

"Not quite yet," Dad said. "We're still drinking in the view. But I'm wondering if we could have a table back a bit from the windows. It's a little too awesome here."

The waitress laughed. "No problem. Some people fight to get these tables, and some people fight to get away from them. I've got a nice little booth back there on solid ground."

42 - The People in the Mirror

Chapter V
Beauty & Disaster

I had never, ever known two-and-a-half days could possibly go so fast. It was wonderful and also kind of sad. It was wonderful, because Mom and Dad got all romancy, and they were so happy they kept hugging me as if they'd just made me all over again. And it was sad, because everything was so-o-o romantic, and here I was, all alone. Not even a sort of boyfriend to dream about—just the neighbor, a complete and total stranger.

But it was good to take a break from the spooky mirror. That mirror didn't seem nearly so disconcerting or important, or even real, here in magic-land at the ocean.

I spent two glorious days doing nothing much other than breathing deeply and walking through the woods or along the beach. On Sunday, early in the afternoon after we'd lingered over brunch, we took the flight of steep and rugged steps down to the ocean and walked along the shore. It would be the last time to take this walk until I returned some unknown day in the future.

The shear face of the rocks rose up beside me, and the fantastic shapes of the ancient evergreens were intertwined, leaning out over the precipice overhead. A foghorn hooted from somewhere across the water like a giant, lonely owl, the sound carried across the cottony fog as if it was a carefully wrapped gift. The whole picture, bathed in a scent that gave me prickly skin, was exciting, so wild and strange, with the evergreens and damp earth and seaweed and sea air.

Mom and Dad walked ahead of me, arms wrapped around each other, their hair blowing in the wind. They looked sooo beautiful—totally like a perfume ad. Just watching them here, in this magical place, touched a soft spot in me, and I found myself walking along with tears rolling down my cheeks. They were so completely in love with each other!

Suddenly I understood something I'd never known before about LOVE. Really real love—how all the arguments and differences of opinion and different wants and likes and don't wants and don't likes— didn't, in the end, matter very much. It was all part of the tension that made each person interesting to the other.

It answered a big question that had bothered me about why I had an obsession to be in love with someone, when relationships looked as though they were more work and pain than they were worth.

But it wasn't more work and pain than it was worth as long as two people loved one another. Somehow, in some strange way, love was a particular kind of glue that made all the other pieces of the puzzle of two different people fit together. It was more than glue, even. It was a kind of mortar, filling up holes and softening hard corners.

WOW!

That was a lot to learn on a lazy Sunday afternoon.

Dad turned and looked over his shoulder at me. "Angel-girl, what's the matter?"

Mom turned too, and they both hurried up to me. My face was wet with tears.

"Oh! Noth-nothing. I was just thinking." How could I explain? I wasn't sure I understood it myself.

"Thinking what? Why are you crying?" Mom put her arm around my shoulders.

"Well, just—you know—the two of you are so beautiful and happy and, like, into each other, and I—I—you looked like a perfume ad. And the day, and about love—and stuff, you know ...."

Mom and Dad looked at each other and back to me. Dad nodded. "We know."

"A perfume ad! That's pretty flattering." Mom definitely liked that picture.

The three of us continued to walk along the shore, arm in arm, with me in the middle just like when I was a little girl and I didn't care who saw us. Not that there was anyone here.

Way too soon, we were back at the lodge packing our things. We were quiet, and the reluctance to leave hung heavily between us. As we piled into the car and took one last lingering look at the lodge, Dad said quietly, "Don't worry old lodge, we'll be back soon enough."

On the way back to the city, I fell into a lovely sleep world where I walked along the moody, stormy, ocean shore, but I wasn't with my parents. I was with the beautiful and sad-eyed boy next door.

And this time we looked like *we* were in a perfume ad.

*   *

When we got to the apartment building it was dark and raining. The parking structure felt cold and depressing. My mood moved into a dark place too. Not only did I feel like I wasn't ready for the heavenly weekend to be over, but there was some other dark thing. I could feel deep into my cold bones that something wasn't right.

Homer opened the front door, pleasant and polite as always, and the foyer was warm and smelled delicately of fresh flowers. There was a comfortable familiarity in walking up to the elevator and pushing '7.' But I still felt deeply that something was wrong.

"Mom?" I asked as we rode up, "do you feel something? Like, something's not right?"

"You're just tired, Sweetheart."

The doors opened. The hall was warmer and looked even more comforting than the foyer.

"Yeah. Must be I'm tired."

Dad started to put the key in the lock, but the door swung open when he touched it. We stepped inside.

"*Robbed!*" Mom whispered, while Dad threw down the luggage, got out his phone, and dialed 911.

Chapter VI
Robbed!

I flew to my room and grabbed my jewelry box. Trembling, I sat on the edge of my bed and opened the box. It was still full of my trinkets, but everything was shifted around, and the hidey hole stood wide open and empty. *"Oh no!"* I wailed, clutching the box.

Mom hurried into my room, followed by Dad. "The police are on their way," he said. Then he looked at me. "Oh! They got Grammy's emerald."

I couldn't say a word, I just nodded. A cold wave of shock and loss rolled over me. It didn't matter what anyone said, I could not, and I *would* not, be consoled. I couldn't bear to lose Grammy again. That's what it felt like. How could I live with myself? Why hadn't I listened to Mom and put the ring in the bank safety box? I was overwhelmed with guilt and a sadness that felt like an unreachable pain.

A minute later I heard Homer come into the living room. Dad and Homer's voices rumbled in serious tones, and then the police pounded at the door. Dad and Homer and the police poked and prodded around.

They eventually all crammed into my room. The policeman told me I shouldn't have touched anything. This made me start to cry in earnest. It was all too unbearably awful. Through my own fault I lost the most important thing in the world to me, and then through my own stupidity, I made it harder to be found.

The policewoman shooed the men out of the room and closed the door. She was kind, and asked me questions about Grammy's ring. She made me feel hopeful.

"I'm so sorry your ring got stolen," she said, "I'll keep an eye out for it myself. I comb the pawn shops from time to time, let's hope it turns it up."

I felt a small ray of hope. "Really? You mean, that's possible?"

"Well—don't get your hopes up. I'm sorry to say that antique jewelry often gets stripped for the gemstones and the gold, but once in a while stuff gets moved in its original setting. We'll just have to hope. Do you have a picture of the ring?"

"Yes. I have a picture of me wearing it." I dug through a photo album. "Here it is. My grandmother let me put the ring on, and I had Dad take a picture. I was about five there."

The policewoman studied the picture for a minute and handed it back to me.

"You don't want to hang on to it?"

"I know now what the ring looks like. An emerald that size will be hard to miss, if ...."

"If what?" I asked, knowing the policewoman meant if they haven't broken down the stone and melted the gold.

"Nothing. Like I said, let's hope for the best."

We went into the foyer where the policeman, Homer, Mom, and Dad were talking.

"What's strange," the policeman was saying, "is that there's absolutely no indication of breaking and entering, no prints anywhere, no jimmied locks, no nothing. Just a really clean job. But we'll keep our eyes open. Good thing the owner had that photo record of the furniture and art. Just shows how important record-keeping is. Don't hesitate to call if anything turns up that we missed."

And they were gone.

After the door closed behind them, Mom and Dad and I looked at one another, tired and discouraged.

"Well," Mom said, "Tomorrow's a school day. You'd better get unpacked and go to bed. Let's not worry about something we can't do anything about right now. At least everything is insured."

I was too depressed and exhausted to say anything. I picked up my luggage and stumbled to my room. closed my door, then went into the bathroom, closed that door too, and turned on the shower. Then I curled up on the bathroom floor, crying, as the room filled with steam. The image of Grammy's emerald being hammered into a dozen pieces was more painful than I could endure.

I finally dragged myself to bed and fell into a fitful sleep. But I woke up with a start when I heard someone calling my name. My bedroom felt warm and had a cozy glow.

"Nikki," Grammy said. She stood in the far corner of the room, her gentle face beaming with the softest illumination and her whole body looking not only like she was standing in a fabulous kind of light, but as if she *was* the light.

"Grammy," I whispered. I wanted to fly from the bed into her arms, but my body behaved as if made of warm molasses syrup and refused to move.

"Don't be unhappy, Dear Heart, the ring is not me, neither is it my love for you. My love will last through eternity. I can't explain how that is, but trust me. However, I want to tell you that the ring will be returned to you. Now sleep and don't worry. And never, never think that you've lost me. I'm where ever you are."

The image of Grammy started to fade, and although I wanted to beg her not to leave, I couldn't speak a word. The warmth of the syrupy feeling stole into my brain, putting me into the deepest, calmest sleep I could ever remember—or not remember—having.

Chapter VII
Wise Counsel

Tom had to shake me awake the next morning, but even then, I still felt the presence of Grammy, and the warmth of her light, into my very bones. That sensation lingered on, even when the missing ring and the robbery and everything came back to me. "Poor Nikki, I guess you're pretty worn out from all the drama."

"But Mom, I saw ...." I stopped. I realized that not only would Mom not believe that I'd seen Grammy, she'd worry like crazy about my mental condition. And I realized I didn't want to tell anyone about Grammy's appearance. At least, not now. "... I mean, I had a dream that I got Grammy's ring back. I feel it in my bones."

"Because I know it means so much to you, I hope you're right," Mom said, giving me a hug. "But Sweetie, don't get you're hopes up too high...."

"I won't, Mom. Well, I'd better get ready for school."

The feeling that lingered after seeing Grammy, and the calm assurance from her that I would get my ring back, lasted all day.

On the way home, I decided to stop and chat with Mr. Zingas. He had talked my ear off one day, telling me the local folklore about how the building we lived in, and particularly the seventh floor, was haunted.

The little bell over the door rang with an old-fashioned cheeriness as I crossed the threshold. The smell of fresh bread and sweet pastries, mixed with the tang of cheeses, comforted me. There were no customers in the store. Mr. Zingas was occupying himself with a feather duster and a top shelf of dust. He looked down at me, then brought his chubby body down the step ladder. "I heard about your family's misfortune. I'm so very sorry."

"Thank you, Mr. Zingas. Well, it does seem pretty lousy that the moment a family goes away for a couple of days, someone comes in and takes everything. I mean, why couldn't they have done that before we moved in? The place was vacant for months, and it doesn't seem quite fair."

Mr. Zingas nodded sympathetically, and as he did so, he cut a couple of slices of cheesecake and motioned me to join him at one of the little deli tables in the back of the store. "Hot tea? The water's ready."

"I'd love it." I heaved a sigh. It was great how he seemed to know just what I needed. "You should be a therapist."

"Exactly, Nikki." He brought two cups of steaming tea to the table. "I'm my own kind of therapist, which is why I'm in the business of food—comforting and nurturing. I can listen, I can talk. But always, I have food and the drink, if needed. I see you need the whole treatment."

I cracked half a smile and nodded. "Well, yes. In fact, I came by because I'm really curious now about that stuff you started to tell me once about my building, especially my floor, being haunted. At that time I just thought of it as stories, but now ... well, here's the thing, the police are really mystified because there's not a sign anywhere of breaking and entering. They have no idea how anyone got in. And I've been puzzling over that all day. How can it be that professionals, who look at ripped off places every day, can't find one single clue? Pretty strange, isn't it?"

"So you're thinking that some ghosts decided to fence some furniture and pictures?"

"Jeez, it doesn't make much sense when you say it out loud, does it?"

Mr. Zingas shrugged. "I try not to pass judgment on how those on the other side reason things out. It's beyond me. But taking a lot of antique furniture and pictures does seem strange. I mean, if they're ghosts, and they live there already, why would they want to move out the furniture?"

"Yeah. Why? So it must be real live people who took everything. But how?"

"A provocative question, young lady. I guess you're not so much wanting to hear ghost stories right now?"

The little bell over the door tink-tinkled.

"I do want to hear them—sometime. But you've managed to help me think along other lines.

Thanks for the tea and cheesecake. It's great brain-food."

Mr. Zingas nodded and winked, then got up to help the woman hovering at the deli counter. At that moment, a buzzer in the back of the store went off and I could hear someone coming through the back door of the shop.

"That you, Alex?"

"Yeah, Dad."

"Come in here and keep Nikki company for a few minutes."

"I've got that delivery."

"It can wait."

"It can wait?" There was incredulity in the young man's voice. He stepped through the bead curtain. "Oh! Hi there."

"Hi," I said back.

"You're in my World Lit class," we said together, then laughed.

He extended his hand, "Hi, Nikki."

I shook his hand, happy to meet the sandy-haired boy who sat in the back of class and occasionally made quiet wisecracks that made everyone laugh. Fortunately, that often included the teacher. "Hi, Alex."

He sat down where his dad had been sitting and picked up his dad's tea and started sipping it like it was the most natural thing in the world to do.

"That's your dad's tea."

"What's his is mine. So, do you live nearby?"

"Yeah." I pointed at the building which could just be seen through the little high up window.

From where we were, we could only see one of its fantastic gargoyles.

"Oh. That place."

"Hmmm ... yes, that place. What does that mean?"

"Just ..." He shrugged. "What floor do you live on?"

"Seventh."

"Cool!" he said like I couldn't have given a better answer.

"Yeah? Why?"

"Okay, no ghostie stories," Mr. Zingas said, returning and taking his tea from Alex. "They were robbed last night."

"Oh! You were the ones robbed?"

"Yeah. Us."

His mood changed completely from the kid who was about to make a bunch of jokes, to someone who sincerely cared. "That's awful I'm sorry to hear it."

"Thank you. It *is* awful. But you dad has made me feel a lot better with his 'medicine.'" I pointed at my empty plate, "And his wise counsel."

"My Dad? Are you sure?" Alex was back into his teasing mode.

Mr. Zingas snapped Alex's ear with his forefinger. "Show respect, young man.'

"Yes, sir," Alex saluted. There was nothing but pure affection between them.

"Thank you. Thank you both for making me feel better. I suppose I'd better get home." I finished my tea and stood.

"See you tomorrow," Alex said.

"Yeah. Cool. See you tomorrow!" Boy, it felt great to be able to say that. I hurried home thinking this would be a huge entry in the GOOD side of my GOOD–BAD lists.

As I came through the door of the apartment, Mom stood in front of me, clearly waiting for the elevator to ding to announce my arrival. She held her fists out in front of her. "Guess which hand," she said with a huge grin, just like she used to do when she had a special treat for me when I was little.

I pointed at Mom's right hand. She opened it, and there sat Grammy's emerald ring!

I squealed in delight, grabbed the ring and kissed it. "Where did you find it?"

"Right on top, in your jewelry box, silly girl. You must have been so scared that the ring was gone, that you shuffled everything around, and buried it without even noticing. I decided to look for it, because it didn't make sense to me that it was missing. I mean, everything else that was gone was furniture and paintings. Thank goodness they didn't take the piano."

"Yeah, Mom, like they could move a baby grand out real subtly."

"Well, anyway, I didn't have any jewelry missing, in fact, my jewelry box hadn't even been touched. So that's what made me think to look for your ring myself. And there it was. I should have known we couldn't get rid of the ugly thing."

I was so stunned by her finding the ring in the

jewelry box that I didn't even argue. But one thing I knew for sure, the ring had not been in my jewelry box. How had it re-materialized? Had Grammy somehow done that? Made her ring come back to me, where it was supposed to be?

"Well, now that the two of you are reunited," Mom continued, "I need you to pick up a few things for me that I forgot to get earlier. I tell you, I can't think straight with the house empty of furniture, and all the activity of the police and everything. Here's a list."

I took the list. "Why didn't you text me?"

"I wanted to surprise you with the ring."

"Oh, yeah. Good job, Mom. You really did surprise me. I guess Mr. Zingas is going to get his fill of me today."

"What do you mean?"

"I just came from there on the way home from school to, ahm, to pick his brain. About what he knows about the neighborhood, you know, and the people. To see if he had any ideas about what might have happened, who might have done the robbery. He's lived here forever."

"And did he know anything?"

"He knew we were robbed and was very sympathetic, but he didn't tell me anything I don't know. His son, Alex, was there. And guess what? He's in my World Lit class. And we talked and he's really nice."

"That's wonderful Nikki," Mom said, but in that distracted way, like she heard me but it didn't register that I had actually talked with a peer. She carried on about the robbery. "I'm still hopeful that the police'll come up with something. They struck me as pretty savvy last night."

"Yeah. The policewoman was very sweet." I went to my room, closed the door, closed the closet door, closed the bathroom door and pulled the shades, then, in the darkness, I hid Grammy's ring in a place where I hoped I could find it again. I ran back out to the living room and picked up the money Mom left for the groceries. "I'll be right back," I hollered over Mom's arpeggiated scales.

Just as the elevator doors closed, I heard a door down the hall open. Once out on the street and heading for Mr. Zingas' store, I looked over my shoulder. There was the gorgeous boy from next door! He acted as if he didn't see me, but his long legs gained on me, and he entered the store right behind me. I felt my heart race, while everything around me seemed to recede. What did Mom want me to get? I looked down at the list. Okay, orange juice. I moved to the cooler. There he stood.

Horrors, I thought, he'll think I'm chasing him. But wait, I came into the store first, and getting orang juice is no big deal, millions of people do it every day. But millions of people do not have to walk around someone who makes their heart stop just to look at him, in order to wrap their hand around a carton of juice.

He stood studying cartons of beverages as if they were the headlines. I waited for him to pick one, when I saw him catch my reflection in the glass. He turned.

"Hi," He said. Very straight-forward and almost like he knew me.

"Hi. Excuse me, I need ...." I gestured at the orange juice.

"Sorry." He stepped aside and I reached in and grabbed any old carton of juice. Was he nervous too?

"My name's Mitch," he said. "I ... I think we're neighbors. Didn't your family recently move in...."

"On the seventh floor? Yes, we're neighbors." I was really glad we were standing by the coolers because I felt myself getting warmer and warmer like I always did when I was shy or embarrassed—or, apparently, infatuated. And I was all three right now. What to say?

"Yes," he continued. "I saw you. I wanted to, I mean, it seemed like—you seem like a nice person, someone I'd like to know."

There was just a hint of an accent to his voice, but I couldn't place it. It was so faint, but it was ancient and warm and lovely. And there was that cologne of his, wafting toward me now in such close proximity it made me weak in the knees. "Well, ah, thank you," I stammered. "I don't know how you can know how I seem, you've only just seen me in the hall."

"I can tell a lot from hearing a person's tone of voice, watching how she moves and seeing how she treats her parents. Actually, I was going for a walk last Friday morning when you and your parents loaded up the car in the parking structure. So, I must confess, I watched you then."

EUGH! I thought. Eugh, eugh, *eugh!* Me, half-asleep, my hair every-which-way, no make-up and in my ugly old sweats. It's a miracle he's even talking to me.

"What's wrong?" he asked. "Are you angry that I watched you? You were right out in public."

"No, I'm not angry that you watched me, I'm just upset that you saw me."

"I don't understand."

"I don't look my best at six a.m., as a rule."

"Oh, you're very wrong. You were so cute, like a little girl, tired and excited about the trip. And your father—is he your father?...."

I nodded.

"Yes, I was sure of it, your father teasing you so sweetly. It was charming." But his voice was sad.

I nodded again, putting the orange juice in my basket, my fingers cold and stiff. "But ... you seem sad."

"Oh! Do I? ... I guess it made me a bit sad. My father died five years ago. We were never close like that, but still ...."

"I'm sorry." There, I thought, there is the reason for the sadness in his eyes.

"Thank you. But now is not the time to be sad. I've finally talked with you, and I'm happy. I have to get some things for my mother, then perhaps we could walk back together?"

"Yes. I have to get some things for my mother too. I'd love to walk back with you."

I quickly got everything on Mom's list, and if it all wasn't exactly what Mom had written, well, it was close enough, wasn't it? I went up to the cash register where Mr. Zingas was ringing up someone else's purchases. "You just can't seem to get rid of me today, can you?" I laughed.

"Not to worry, I enjoy your company," he answered. But something was strange about him as he rang up my purchases, somehow he was distracted. Just as he finished, Mitch came and stood behind me.

"What's ...." I was going to say to Mr. Zingas "bothering you," but as I watched his eyes narrow ever so slightly as he glanced at Mitch, I switched my sentence in mid-stream to, "what's my total?"

"Fourteen-twenty-one." Mr. Zingas answered in a nothing-but-business-going-on-here tone of voice. I handed over a ten and a five and received back my change without so much as a wink. That was entirely un-Mr. Zingas like. Great mystery.

Goodness, I thought, I'll have to come back and see him a third time tonight just to find out what's going on. I stood by the door and thumbed through a magazine while Mitch bought his groceries, but really I was watching what was going on between Mr. Zingas and Mitch. Which appeared to be exactly nothing. But Mr. Zingas was certainly not friendly to Mitch.

As we stepped out into the swiftly falling night, I couldn't resist wondering aloud what was wrong between the two of them. "Why did Mr. Zingas treat you so coldly?"

"He did? I didn't notice. He seemed the same as always."

"He's never friendly with you, never tells you jokes or stories about his wife and children?"

"Never! Does he do that with you?"

"Yes, always, until just now."

Mitch laughed. It was a beautiful laugh, and his bright, white teeth made me fall from infatuation into something deeper with a crash. "I have no trouble believing that a middle-aged man would spend time telling a pretty, intelligent, curious, and charming young woman stories and jokes, while not having any particular interest in doing the same with some teenage boy."

"But he does it with my Dad too."

"And Dad is the source of the cash flow, no?"

"Yes." I thought about what Mitch said, and it almost made sense. Except for that fleeting look Mr. Zingas had given Mitch. That was clearly not neutral.

When we got to the front door of the apartment, Homer nodded and smiled. "I was wondering when you two young people would get to know one another. Aren't you about the same age?"

"I'm fifteen," I said, dying of curiosity over what Mitch was about to say.

"Well, I guess I'm about sixteen, although celebrating birthdays is not something we do in our family."

I didn't say anything until we were on the elevator, alone. "No birthdays? Why?"

"My great-great-grandfather, who, by the way, built this building, said that celebrating birthdays was how one grew older, and that if one was just oneself, one needn't get old in the same way as everyone else."

I had never heard of such a philosophy. "I—I'll have to think about that for a while. It's very interesting, but I don't think I'm ready to give up birthdays just yet—there's the pay-off of presents. I have to imagine what it would be like not to get any more birthday presents." We were standing in the hall outside my apartment when Mom flung the door open.

"Oh. Well, I thought I heard your voice. I thought you were talking to yourself, but I couldn't understand why you didn't just come on in."

"Thanks, Mom."

"What?"

"You make me sound sort of like a lunatic."

"Everyone talks to themselves, it's no big deal."

"Your mother's right," Mitch agreed.

Mom gave Mitch a studied look. "I've seen you before, haven't I?"

"Mom, this is Mitch, he's our neighbor. I think he lives in the next apartment."

"I see. Well, it's nice to meet you, Mitch. Did you get robbed too?"

"What do you mean?"

"We were robbed over the weekend, and I was wondering if you were too?"

Mitch fidgeted. I watched his metamorphosis from coolness to discomfort in amazement. "No, ah no. We weren't. But we ... ah, ahm ... we don't have nice things like you do, that is, the Rionews. I hope you—or they—have insurance. I saw all the commotion the other night, and I felt bad for all of you."

"Did you?" I asked. "That's so sweet."

"Actually," Mitch went on, gathering his previous cool self, "I'm pretty familiar with a lot of the furniture in your apartment, since I've visited the Rionews on occasion. I'll keep my eyes open for it, in case it gets fenced anywhere nearby. Well, It's been very nice meeting you Mrs.—oh, I'm not sure I know your last name?"

"Francis," Mom and I said together.

"Mrs. Francis. And I look forward to having another interesting talk with you, Nikki." Mitch went on down the hall.

"Cute boy," Mom said. "Almost too cute." She took the bag of groceries from me and hustled into the kitchen.

"What do you mean?" I tried hard to sound oh-so-casual, as I helped Mom put away the groceries.

"You know what I mean. Listen, Dad called while you were getting groceries and one of his co-workers insists on taking us out to dinner, so get dressed. Dad said he'll be home," Mom glanced at the clock, "well, anytime now."

I shuddered at the thought. Dinner with adult strangers in a restaurant, trapped in one spot. Anyway, I wanted to go back down and ask Mr. Zingas what was up with that look he gave Mitch. "But, Mom, can't I just stay here and do my homework, and stuff?" I begged.

"No, Nikki. Your dad said they have a daughter about your age and the idea is to get the two 'families' together. They're taking us to some elegant place that's on the water with a fabulous view. So make the best of it. Dress nice."

Nice. I pulled myself down the hall to my room and into my closet. Nice meant ... well, maybe my little plaid dress with the white collar and knee sox. Actually, although I probably wouldn't admit it to any of my "cool" friends in Laguna Beach, I was fond of this outfit, one of several Mom and I had gotten for me when we first moved here. Trying to dress for the climate.

There was something about the blue tartan, with its interweaving of dark blues and greens with a flash of red, yellow and white, that fascinated me. Especially if I was bored, I could just contemplate how these threads ran this way and those ran that way, over and under, and the crossings made sort of other colors. It was pretty interesting.

I heard Dad come in the front door, hurry into the master bath and start the shower. Mom and Dad talked back and forth while they got ready. I could tell that Dad was "briefing" her on what he knew about the people we were about to have dinner with.

I hoped with all my might that the daughter who was "the same age" as me wasn't two or three years younger. Why didn't adults understand that "about the same age" meant someone who was born within nine or ten months of you, and who was in the same grade in school. And sometimes even then ....

"Come on, Nikki, we're ready, let's go." Mom called. I reluctantly joined them in the living room.

Mom was wearing one of her "quiet black dresses," as she called them, and Dad had put on a suit exactly like the one he left in that morning.

"Oh, Nikki, good choice." Mom smiled. "You look darling."

Darling. Well, at least she didn't say "cute."

"You look great too, Mom." Sophisticated, I wanted to say. And sure of herself. How did she know how to do all of that? I'd never be so together.

On the ride to the restaurant I tried to imagine what it would be like if, for instance, I was an adult, with Mitch, off to some adult function.

"You're awful quiet," Mom said. "Thinking about the neighbor boy?"

"No, I'm not thinking about the neighbor boy," I half-lied. After all, I was mostly thinking about Mom.

"What neighbor boy?" Dad looked at me in the rear view mirror, which I always found very disconcerting. It was like Dad really did have eyes in the back of his head.

"Nikki came home with a boy appended tonight," Mom said, "I embarrassed her to death because I could hear her talking in the hall and when she didn't come in, I opened the door to ask her what she was doing, and there was this dangerously good-looking boy listening to her with undivided attention. Nikki says he's our immediate neighbor. He only said a few words, but he has this very subtle eastern European accent. Very charming, lilting. Sexy, to be quite frank."

"Well, jeez Mom, you want me to ask him if he wants to go out with you?"

"No thanks, sweetie, I've got all the man I can handle," Mom pinched Dad's cheek. "I don't need any little boys."

"So, how long have you known this 'dangerously good looking, sexy' package of trouble?"

"Well, let's see, it's seven-thirty, so I guess about two hours."

"He lives next door, but you just met him?"

"Umm-hum. I've seen him a couple of times, but tonight he came into Mr. Zingas' store when I was there and introduced himself to me, because he'd seen me and knew we were neighbors, and we walked back together. End of report. Shall I sign in blood? And how often am I required to file an update?"

"My, my, we hit a nerve," Dad observed.

"Well, it's a bit much, isn't it, that I can't have a civilized conversation with a neighbor without said neighbor being accused of being dangerous? Can't a person be good-looking without being treated like it's some sort of handicap? He's very polite and interesting, so it seems to me the least one could do is be polite in return. By the way, his great-great-grandfather built the building we live in. For what that's worth."

"Really? Very interesting. Well, Puss-Boots, you're absolutely right, and I stand corrected. I look forward to meeting our interesting, polite neighbor, who happens, by total coincidence, and without fatherly prejudice and concern, to be good-looking." Dad pulled into a driveway leading to a restaurant with a subdued nautical motif. "Here we are. Hey, this place looks great!"

Dad parked the car. We all got out and approached the entrance.

"Where's the daughter?" I asked as we walked up to three people smiling at us.

"I assume that's her, on the right."

"Well, how old is she?"

"Eighteen, I think, I don't remember exactly."

"Oh, great," I said under my breath. There was no time for further conversation as the introductions were made. The girl's name was Stephanie.

Stephanie had absolutely nothing to say to me. She had just started at the University of Washington—a college woman. It was much worse than trying to hang out with someone younger than me. Here I am, with all these attractive women, in my little white collar and knee sox. Jeez. The final humiliation.

I salvaged the evening by enjoying the fabulous view and thinking about how much my fortune had turned for the better. I had met two interesting young men in one evening. And I had gotten Grammy's ring back. Despite my internal awkward feelings around the beautiful and svelte Stephanie, I rejoiced in getting Grammy's ring back.

A myriad lights reflected in the rippling water as I turned over in my mind what Mom had so off-handedly said about Mitch's accent being eastern European. Wasn't that just entirely romantic?

Chapter VIII
Double Bind

Somehow I survived the humiliation of the dinner. Anyway, Dad was apparently elated by whatever he'd accomplished with Mr. Turner during dinner, who was his supervisor at work. Dad sang show tunes all the way home, no matter how much Mom and I, *captive audience!*, protested and begged him to stop.

His mood was contagious, and by the time we pulled into the parking garage, Mom and I had decided that if you couldn't beat him, you'd have to join him, and we were singing at the top of our lungs with the grand finale of "There Ain't Nothing Like a Dame" when Dad shut the engine off.

The requirement to become civilized and quiet had us all giggling by the time we arrived at the front door. There was one of the non-Homer doormen at the door, and he looked at us as if he suspected us of indulging in too much of something.

We tip-toed down the hall after getting off the elevator, and once inside the apartment, permitted one grand guffaw to get it out of our systems.

"Okay, munchkin," Dad said, "School in the morning, off to bed."

"Munchkin! Yeah, that's me. By the way, Dad, a girl who's eighteen and a freshman in college is not about my age, you know?"

"What? ... You mean Stephanie? I guess the two of you didn't have much in common, did you? But you seem so mature to me, I thought for sure someone a bit older than you wouldn't matter."

"Three years, Dad. I mean, thanks for the vote of confidence, or whatever it is, but I hope to think that when I'm a freshman in college I'll ... I'll be a lot more, you know, more ... more like Stephanie. I hope."

"But you behaved like an adult tonight, and I'm completely proud of you. Especially if you were uncomfortable. I didn't see it, which proves my point. And you were there for your old Dad. Thanks and go to sleep."

"You're welcome and I'm gone."

I followed my dreams into a land where I danced with a prawn on the rippling surface of the ocean, until Mitch cut in and danced with me inside a dusky mirror. I looked up and saw myself watching me dance with Mitch in an ancient hall, with piano music swelling to the walls and pouring out through the mirror into my closet.

*　*

The next morning, when I dragged myself into the kitchen, Mom was all atwitter because the police had called and said they'd found a couple of small pieces of furniture at a pawn shop, and that once a couple things turned up, more usually followed.

"That's great, Mom. This barren, echo-y place was starting to get on my nerves."

"You and me both, but the worst of it for me has been the horror of facing the Rionews. Dad talked with Mr. Rionews, and he said he took the disaster very well, but I just want to get their things back, if at all possible."

"Me too. It'd be great to come home from school to a furnished apartment."

The news about the furniture was fantastic, but I was still more preoccupied with wondering when I'd get to see Mitch again. Did I have to rely on accidental, coincidental meetings in the hall or in the corner grocery? I already knew I could go for days without seeing him, if that were the case. On the other hand, I couldn't imagine gathering the courage to walk down the hall and knock on his door.

But there he was, talking with Homer at the front door of the building when I came home from school that afternoon. He fell into step beside me, and we rode up in the elevator, just as if we'd planned it.

"How was school?"

"Okay," I answered, unable to resist asking one of my biggest questions. "Where do you go to school?"

"I don't. I've done home study since my father died. I live with my mother and my uncle—my dad's brother. We moved in with him when my father passed, and he sort of rules us with an iron hand. He told my mother he didn't want a cookie cutter kid for a nephew, which is how he feels about public school. Sorry, no insult meant."

"None taken," I replied, studying his dark eyes that looked away from me in discomfort. Oh, my, he was so beautiful!

"He never went to school at all. He has the idea that it's something awful."

"Wow," I said, for lack of anything more profound. "How do you feel about it?"

"Sometimes it's okay because both my uncle and my mom teach me, and they know a lot. But sometimes I'd like to be with people my own age. My family is Romanian and they have a long heritage of sticking with family, no matter what. I mean, whether they're right or wrong. It goes back generations, so who am I to even consider breaking the chain?

"But sometimes chains get old and rusty and they don't serve anymore."

We come to the seventh floor and were now standing in front of my apartment. Talking in the hall again! I hoped Mom wouldn't pop her head out the door, as seemed to be her new habit.

"What do you mean?"

"I mean I want to go to college, I want to break family tradition. I want to study law, and, perhaps become a lawyer."

"What does your uncle want you to become?"

"Oh, ah, well, it's kind of hard to explain. I'll ... we'll get into that some other time."

I sensed yet more discomfort from Mitch and let the subject drop. "Do you want to come in and, I don't know, talk some more?"

Right then Mom started playing the piano and the round tones of scales muffled their way through the door.

"Your mother is a wonderful pianist."

"Scales?"

"Anything. She's got the touch of an artist. I'll tell you, I'd rather listen to your mother play scales for an hour than have any of the Rionews attempt to play for five minutes. There's no escaping hearing your piano in our apartment, but with your mother playing, I never want to escape it."

"I can't imagine any way more directly to my Mom's heart than for her to hear that kind of praise. Come on in. You can sit on the sofa and listen to her play without the walls between. I'll even bring you milk and cookies, not-cookie-cutter boy."

Grinning like a little boy on his birthday, Mitch followed me inside. And, well, of course Mom was crazy flattered when he told her how much he enjoyed her playing.

"What would you like to hear?" she asked, fingers poised over the keys.

"I love all the classical composers," Mitch said, working his way ever deeper into Mom's heart. Then he made the last parry by saying, "But Beethoven is my favorite."

Mom's too.

I was happy to wait on Mitch and share his enjoyment of the spontaneous piano concert. After half-an-hour, Mom quit and stretched, smiling at us. She pointed to the far wall. "Didn't you notice, Nikki?"

I hadn't even looked around the apartment, I was so engrossed in Mitch. "Oh! Look, that painting is back! That's wonderful. I guess the police are on top of things."

I watched out of the corner of my eye as Mitch nervously looked at his watch. He leapt up. "Goodness, I didn't realize it was so late, I've got to get home. Thank you for letting me listen to you play, Mrs. Francis, I enjoyed it more than I can express." And he bolted from the apartment.

Mom and I exchanged a that-was-sort-of-weird look. I felt disappointment creeping over me that I didn't get to talk with him more. I mean, we just listened to Mom play. Why didn't he say, "I'll see you tomorrow after school," or "do you want to do something this weekend?" Or something. Or anything.

But then, if his peer group socialization was curtailed as much as he'd said, how would he know what the girl next door might hope he'd do or say? I suddenly realized he seemed more at ease talking with Mom than with me.

"Charming young man, really," Mom mused. "Do you know any more about him than you did before?"

"His family is Romanian, so you were right about the accent. His father died five years ago, and now he and his mother live with his uncle. Oh, and his uncle keeps him out of public school because he doesn't want Mitch to be a 'cookie-cutter boy' like everyone who goes to public school. He wants to be a lawyer, but his uncle doesn't want him to become that, either, it seems. He said his uncle never went to school at all."

"Hmmm," Mom said cautiously. "The uncle sounds sort of like a tyrant."

"Yeah. That's what I think."

"By-the-by, Nikki, don't forget your appointment with Dr. Carcionne tomorrow."

"What a segue, Mom! From tyrant to shrink. How could I 'forget' something I didn't know about? I'm doing great, Mom, I don't need to see her."

"It can't hurt to go a few times. There must be things you could use a sounding board to help you sort out."

"I've got you and Dad, Mom. My over-protective parents."

"I'm glad you feel that you can talk with us," she said, ignoring the "overprotective" part. "And I have to admit, I'm very happy to see you making some positive adjustments to your new environment. But this business of being robbed, and the trauma you went through when you thought your ring was missing—I don't want you to be scarred."

"I'm not scarred, Mom. I've got my ring, and I'm fine."

"That's good. I hope you share all of that with Dr. Carcionne. Dad is going to pick you up after school to take you to your appointment."

"He's leaving work early?"

"I had planned to take you, but he said he had some errands to run and he'd just take off an hour early and get both birds with one stone, so that's all organized."

"Ah. I'm just a stoned little bird, am I?" Not waiting for Mother to reply, I went to my bedroom and changed into jeans and a sweatshirt, feeling very grouchy about having to see Dr. Carcionne the next day. Then I suddenly realized, too, that I wouldn't be coming home at my usual time, so, if by chance, Mitch was watching for me, he wouldn't see me. Yet another downer.

On the other hand, I decided, I really could use a good talk with someone who didn't have it all decided in her mind what I think, and what I mean, and what I need, like Mom did. If only Dr. Carcionne would be that person!

It still felt like Mom was putting her fears onto me. It was Mom who felt violated and invaded and threatened and afraid since the theft. And, honestly, I couldn't blame her. She didn't have the visitation from Grammy that I'd had that made everything all right.

That's when a wonderful plan sprung full-blown in my mind. I could nab a couple of birdies with a single stone, too!

*　*

Once inside Dr. Carcionne's inner sanctum the next afternoon, I tried to remember exactly what I had rehearsed the night before, but the clever way I'd put it together slipped my mind. Then Dr. Carcionne really messed it up by starting off with her own agenda—or rather, Mom's.

"Your mother mentioned that you've started up a friendship with a neighbor boy."

Something came over me. I wasn't going to tolerate this spying any more. "Look, Dr. Carcionne, it's like this—my Mom feels obligated to force me to come and see you. I'm interested in that being as few times as possible, because you and she have an agenda for me. But it's not my agenda.

"If I can't come in here and talk about what I want to talk about, and if I can't feel like what goes on between us in your office is confidential, then I'm going to be honest and tell you I'm going to clam up. It's that simple.

"But if we can strike a bargain that this is my time, and my agenda, that it's strictly confidential, then I might try to get involved in this process. If not, then ... not."

Dr. Carcionne's eyebrows went up. But, slowly, a smile spread over her face. "I agree with you completely. First, let me reassure you that what little interaction you and I have had has been confidential. I haven't told your mother what we've talked about. She just tells me what her concerns are about you, and, of course, I listen. But I agree with you that these sessions need to serve your needs and interests, not your mother's."

Now it was my turn for my eyebrows to go up. "Wow! That was pretty painless."

"So—what do you want to talk about?"

"Well, if we're going to work on what's important to me, then I have tons of stuff. But at the top of the list is sort of this same subject. Let's say there's a mother who, whenever something happens to her, she has her daughter go to therapy because what's upsetting to the mother she's sure is causing the daughter to freak out.

"But it's not true. The things that are biggest to the daughter, the mother either doesn't think are important, or she doesn't know about them at all.

"So let's say the daughter wishes there was something she could do to help her mother. For instance, when the mother had something stolen, and she's really, really upset about it, instead of admitting that, she tells the daughter, oh, you must be so upset about this theft. You must be unhappy, you must be scarred.

"And the daughter answers that it does make her unhappy, but she's not afraid or angry, and she's certainly not scarred. She's not afraid because she feels protected by her parents, she's not angry because everything that was stolen was insured.

"Not that she doesn't feel awful about it, but she's not silently freaking out. But she does think the mother is quietly freaking out. What could a daughter in a situation like that do to help the mother?"

Dr. Carcionne nodded. I could tell she was really listening.

"I'd suggest to the daughter that she tell the mother in this same direct way what her observations are."

"What if the daughter has done that, and the mother gets all mad because the daughter is acting insubordinate. What if the mother really can't look at her stuff, and, in fact, it gets worse when the daughter tries to say out loud what she feels she's seeing."

"Then I'd say the daughter has been put in an untenable position ... the daughter is in a double bind."

"Yeah. I don't know what that is, but it sounds right to me."

"It's when, no matter what you do, you can't do the 'right' thing because the other person has made all the possible choices 'wrong'—so one can't move in any direction. My next suggestion is that perhaps regarding this one subject the daughter let her therapist address it with the mother, and see if some progress can be made. What do you think of that alternative?"

"Well ... if that can be done very carefully, in order not to cause the mother to make the daughter's life a living hell, like what happened when the therapist told the mother that the daughter accused the mother of projecting."

"Ahh. In that case, I can't blame you for being cautious with me. I wouldn't want to talk with me anymore, either. I have an idea, let's write out a plan and an agreement for what our focus will be for the next few sessions. I'll give this issue surrounding the mother's projection some thought if you don't mind, just letting things settle for the moment."

"I don't mind. As long as I feel someone finally understands my dilemma, I can be very patient about how to solve it."

Chapter IX
The Boy of My Dreams

I couldn't have been more surprised when I walked through the door at home after my appointment with Dr. Carcionne, to hear Mitch in the kitchen, talking with Mom.

"Who's that?" Dad asked.

"Mitch," I answered.

"Hi, guys," Mom called. "Come and join us. Mitch helped me carry in the groceries, and I asked him to stay for dinner. Mitch, this is Nikki's father, Dan."

The two of them shook hands and exchanged greetings. I was delighted to see Mitch, but I felt strangely shy and at a loss for words. I didn't really know Mitch that well, and now here he was, with all of my parents. Like, what could a person say, anyway?

"How was your session?" Mom asked.

Well, that was absolutely not what I wanted to have brought up. "Fine, Mom."

"Really?"

"Actually, yeah, really. But, you know, I don't want to talk about it now."

"That's okay. I already told Mitch where you were when he said he hoped he'd see you after school, but it seemed you didn't come home."

What was okay about telling a boy you liked that you were at a shrink session? I wondered, verging on furious. "First you tell him you think I'm talking to myself in the hall, then you tell him I'm in therapy. You're going to have him scared to even tip-toe past the door for fear of the crazy girl."

Mom laughed. "Nonsense. You're being too sensitive."

"Well," Mitch finally jumped in, "I'm, not afraid of you, and I know you're not crazy. I think the science of the mind is very important," he continued. "And to understand one's mind with the assistance of someone trained in the field is ... wise."

"See?" Mom said. "He's almost got me convinced to make an appointment for myself. After all, you don't have to be dysfunctional to go to therapy. You can want to go and work on gaining insight."

"That's nice that I don't have to be dysfunctional, Mom."

"Oh dear," she said, actually sensitive enough to become a bit flustered. "That didn't come out like I meant it. Get washed up for dinner, it'll be ready soon. Mitch is so helpful. He set the table and everything."

"Thanks," I said to him as I left the kitchen. Well, what else do you say to a boy you like who has just done your chores?

In my room I decided that the whole thing was a little too weird. Just entirely toooo much parent-presence. But I had to make the best of it. I pulled on a pair of jeans, then tried on half-a-dozen tops. Too casual, too ragged-old, ugly color, too dressy. There was no hope for it. I went back to "too casual," the pale blue tee-shirt that sort of matched my eyes. Well, this was me most of the time. Mitch might as well know the real me, casual tee-shirts, shrink sessions, and all.

Dinner was not quite the disaster I'd braced myself for. Mitch, with his adult manner, carried on intelligent, interesting conversation with my parents, but he didn't miss an opportunity to give me the occasional sidelong glance and slightly conspiratorial smile.

We both seemed to understand that conversation between just the two of us was a lost cause, and besides, what I was learning about him through my parents' curiosity was more than I'd ever ask him on my own. I couldn't imagine asking him all these questions about his experiences, his family and his ambitions for the future.

By the time Mom brought out the cheesecake—which reminded me that I still wanted to talk with Mr. Zingas about why he didn't like Mitch—Dad had offered to see what he could do to help Mitch get into college when the time came, or what he needed to do to test out, as he hadn't had an institutional education.

"If you think you could pass college prep exams, I'm willing to go to bat for you," Dad said.

"I've been preparing for them on my own. I have more than one reference book and I've taken a bunch of sample tests. I believe I'll do all right."

"Great! Of course, I wouldn't want to go behind your uncle's back, or have him think that I had, if he's your legal guardian."

"Well, he's not." There was passion in Mitch's voice. I looked at him quickly, it was the first thing like anger I'd seen cross his features. I could tell that Mom and Dad picked up on it too, but Dad just continued.

"Fine. I'll see what I can do. Your ambitions are admirable, and you're obviously very bright, as well as mature. It doesn't seem right for you to be held back when, in some ways, you have it all over most college freshmen."

Mitch got shy. "Well, thanks. It'd mean more to me than I can express. It could make the difference for the whole path of my life."

After the dishes were cleared away and Mitch went down the hall to his home, I felt Dad looking at me.

"What?" I finally said.

"I can see why you find that young man attractive," Dad answered.

"Oh, Da-a-a-d!"

"Your mom is right about him. The little boys you've been interested in up until this point have been, well, boys. But Mitch is an attractive, intelligent, poised young man."

"Are you telling me you don't want me to be friends with him?"

"No, I'm not telling you that. I might as well chain you to your bedpost and never let you out of my sight ever again, as to say that. What I'm saying is ... I'm saying that tonight I've had to take another look at my baby girl, and here I see she's become a young woman. I don't know why you have to grow up so fast Bunny Love, but my job is to be aware, and to remind you that I'm here if you need me."

Dad reached out and took Mom's hand, "that we're here, and you can come to us with anything. Okay?"

My telephone, laying on the entry table rang, which almost never happens, and with gratitude for the interruption, I leapt up to answer it.

"Hi," Mitch said.

"Oh, hi." He must have forgotten something. I looked around to see if there was anything that might be his.

"I forgot to ask you something," he said. "No, that's not true, I didn't forget, I just couldn't ask you with your parents hanging on to every word. I wanted to ask you if you wanted to do something, maybe, on Saturday night. That's when people our age do, go out and do things, right?"

"Yeah, yes, pretty much."

"So, would you?"

"Yes." I turned my back to my parents, with their ears straining almost all the way to my phone.

"What would you like to do? I'm not too familiar with, I mean, I know sometimes there are high school sports that everyone goes to and you wouldn't want to miss it, like basketball."

"Not this weekend, no."

"So, what would you like to do?"

"Anything, really." If you wanted me to go to Safeway and watch you buy canned vegetables, I'd be in heaven, I thought. But I didn't say it.

"Maybe this is a bit embarrassing to admit, but I'd kind of like to see the movie, *The Fairy Godfather*," he said.

"Yeah?" I was surprised. It was an animation, but getting rave reviews. Definitely a step up from spending an evening with him in Safeway. "Well, that's fine with me," I said.

"You don't think I'm like a kid to want to see it?"

"I think we're both sort of kids, and that's okay."

"Well, okay. Great. I'll come to your place at five on Saturday."

"Five?"

"Is there anything wrong with that? I thought if we started the evening early, that'd make it last longer."

Good logic. "Yeah, that's fine. Five."

"And tell your folks thanks again for me, will you?"

"Sure."

"Good night, then."

"Good night." I hung up.

Silence reigned for a few moments, but finally Mom said, "Well?"

"That was Mitch."

"We figured that much."

"He wants to take me to a movie Saturday night."

"And so it begins," Mom said melodramatically. "What movie?"

"You're never going to believe this—he wants to see The Fairy Godfather."

"Isn't that a kid's animation?" Dad asked.

"Yeah."

"Won't you be bored?" Mom asked.

"Nope."

"If we wanted to take you ...."

"Yep, I'd be bored. Well, I'm tired, I'm going to bed. Plus I gotta think about what I'm going to wear Saturday night."

I went to bed, but I didn't think about what I'd wear Saturday night. I only thought about the fact that, somewhere on the opposite side of my wall, probably not fifty feet away, lay the boy of my dreams. I hoped I was in his dreams too.

*　*

Well, finally, the next night after school I found a moment to stop in and see Mr. Zingas. He wasn't too busy, there was only one customer in the store in the back corner going over the reduced dented cans with a fine-toothed budget.

"Hi, Mr. Zingas."

"Hello there, Nikki. What's new? What's with the big smile? You just get your teeth cleaned?"

"Nope. Just happy I guess."

"You wear it well. What makes you so happy?"

"The same thing, er, person, that I came to talk with you about. Mitch, my neighbor. I've been trying to get in here to talk with you since the other day. I saw you give him the worst look that day, and I've been wondering why."

"Mr. Zingas' expression went from jovial to stormy. "Don't ask questions when you may not care for the answers."

"What does that mean?"

"It means I don't trust him, and I don't like his family. They've lived here for generations, and my people have lived here for generations. The fact of the matter is, my people and his people were at odds with one another before we ever came to this country."

"So you're Romanian too?"

"I'm Romanian. I don't know about 'too.'"

"What are you saying?"

"I'm saying Mitch's family has very suspect morals. I wouldn't turn my back on him for one second. Don't forget your place was just robbed."

Shocked, I said, "you're actually accusing Mitch's family of robbing us?!"

Mr. Zingas shook his head. "I wouldn't come right out and say that, no. What I would say is, never turn your back on the ocean."

"Okay. You sound like my mother. But why so cryptic?"

"It's best left at that. Speaking of your mother, she mentioned that the police recovered a couple pieces of furniture and some art."

I nodded. "Yeah. It's great. The place doesn't look quite so empty." I couldn't get Mr. Zingas' disturbing suggestion out of my mind. "But, getting back to Mitch ... I can't imagine him having anything to do with stealing from us. I mean, last night he helped my mother bring in the groceries, and he even set the table. He stayed for dinner. And then he asked me to go to a kid's movie Saturday night." I paused. "What you're suggesting really is too much."

"I'm sorry. I see I've upset you." Mr. Zingas gave me a disconcerting study. He saw something that made him shrug, and he shifted his mood—at least outwardly. "I hope it all works out for you, dear girl, I really do. You know I only wish you the best."

"Thank you, Mr. Zingas. I appreciate your concern." I gave him a little wave as I stepped back out into the night. "Talk to you later."

"Okay, Nikki."

I walked around the block the long way. I wanted to think about this disturbing conversation. I wasn't ready to say hi to Homer, or talk with Mom, or, least of all, run into Mitch. It was apparent that Mr. Zingas knew something he wasn't saying about Mitch and his family. What could it possibly be?

Chapter X
A Great Date

Finally it was Saturday, and despite the feelings of hesitation Mr. Zingas had planted, I looked forward to five o'clock with rising nerves and excitement.

By four I felt sick enough to wonder if I'd even be able to go out at all. I took a hot bath and practiced breathing deeply, as well as doing my best not to think about Mitch at all. Hopeless. It was the combination of powerful emotions, I told myself that caused me the trouble with my system. If Mr. Zingas just hadn't said those bad things about Mitch's family, I'd only have positive emotions and wouldn't feel so awful.

Next, I had to wonder what I should wear. As we were going to an animation, it'd look pretty dumb if I wore something dressy. But I wanted to dress up a little bit. He'd never seen me at my best. And he'd certainly seen me at my worst. On the other hand, there'd always be some occasion to dress up, wouldn't there? Yeah, if tonight I just wouldn't do something truly horrible like throw up in his car, which I felt I might do if my nerves didn't settle down.

I did some more deep breathing, and gradually began to feel better. I decided to wear my baby blue cashmere sweater dress—medium dressy, and everyone always said I looked great in it. I hoped Mitch had the same taste as "everyone."

It was only a few minutes later when I heard the doorbell ring. I took a last look in the mirror, shrugged, squeezed a departing poof of perfume at myself, picked up my purse and jacket and went into the living room.

Mitch was seated on one of the sofas with Mom across from him. He'd just said, "don't you think?" when he looked up at me.

Mom said, "Indeed I do think so! I couldn't agree more," and seemed to be waiting for a response from Mitch, but he was unavailable. He was on a trip to ... well, me.

Yes, it was a wise choice, the baby blue cashmere sweater dress.

"Oh, Nikki," Mom said, "You look beautiful!"

"Yes, you do," Mitch agreed. "Angelic."

"Thank you," I said shyly. "I guess we'd better go as the movie starts pretty soon."

"Yes, we'd better. Mrs. Francis, I look forward to continuing this conversation in the near future. And don't worry about Dominique. I'll have her home by eleven, if that's appropriate."

"Her father will be pleased. Have fun!"

Mitch and I had nothing to say on the elevator ride down and the brief walk to the parking structure. But it wasn't an uncomfortable silence, we both seemed to agree it was just fine if we didn't talk.

"Hope you don't mind our family jalopy," he said quietly.

"Ah, no, I don't care in the least." I wouldn't care if was a little red wagon, as long as we were together. But I didn't say that last part out loud.

At the theatre there were a lot of little kids, and I was afraid we'd be surrounded by them, chattering and leaping about during the movie, and I'd be miserable.

But, magically, Mitch found a niche where there were almost no children, and the few that were there were well-behaved, and I was able to engage in the story as it unfolded on the screen.

I generally didn't care for animation—after all, it's not real, and I liked to watch beautiful, interesting, dangerous, real people. But somehow I got entirely caught up in the story. I had no problem pretending I was watching real people.

It was about a young man, Andrew, searching for his destiny. His father had died, leaving him with property and responsibilities, but he had not left him with a credo. There was a fairy godfather who looked oddly like Mr. Zingas, with a pontificating manner, there was a girl, Serena, in a faraway city who kept dreaming of a young man she would one day meet, who, in her dreams, looked quite a bit like Andrew, except the picture of him was filmy and dreamy.

There were numerous obstacles between Andrew and his "true self" as he made a quest for the deeper meaning of his life. There was a moment when the cartoon Andrew was yelling at his father for leaving him, and I felt Mitch tense up beside me—it seemed he was about to cry. I found myself wishing I could make it all better. But, I realized, like Serena, I could only wait in a "neighboring city" or apartment, until he sorted out his journey.

When the movie was over and we came out of the theatre, I was still so caught up in the story that I wasn't ready to let go of it yet.

"What did you think?" Mitch asked as we walked to the car.

"I think I know why you wanted to see this movie."

He stopped under a street lamp and turned to face me. "Do you really?"

"Sure. The story was like Joseph Campbell writes about the quest of the hero. Andrew had to search outside of himself in order to learn what was inside himself. And his father dying was like symbolic of his lower nature dying, and the godfather was like his higher self calling to him.

"But he was the one who had to do the searching to get from the one to the other. And Serena was symbolic of the feminine characteristics he had to learn to understand and honor, to fulfill his destiny, like his lessons to be patient, and to keep dreaming."

"Wow," Mitch said quietly. "You got more out of the film than I did. I saw the ads for it and knew there was something there that would be meaningful to me.

"I saw some of what you just pointed out, but about the father being the lower self and the

Godfather being the higher self and Andrew going from one to the other, I didn't see that. And your insight that Serena was symbolic of his need to have a balance with his feminine energy, that's good."

I discovered that I was entirely ready for Mitch to lean down and kiss me. But he didn't. He took my hand and led me to the car, not saying another word until we were settled. He turned on some quiet music, and we sat companionably listening to it for a few minutes.

"There's a place I'd love to take you, but I'm afraid you're too dressed up for it. Of course we can go some other time, but it just ties into the film in my mind. I don't understand why exactly, but it feels like it does."

"What sort of place is it?"

"It's where I go when I'm trying to sort out my quest."

"Oh, let's go. Is it in the country?"

"Not exactly. I have some sweats in the trunk if you wanted to put them on. I mean, I love you in this dress, but I wouldn't want you to ruin it if we're to go exploring."

"Well, maybe I could just pull the sweats on over it."

"There's an idea."

Mitch drove us up and down and around, out to the edge of the city. Finally, he stopped the car in a forlorn, abandoned place. "Here we are."

"Where?"

"You'll see." He got out and dug around in the trunk, bringing me a pair of black sweat pants and black sweat shirt. "Jeez, I forgot about your shoes. You can't crawl around in those things."

"That's true. I hadn't planned on crawling around."

"Pull the sweats on, I'll be right back."

I got out of the car and pulled on the sweats thinking, could we have gotten any farther from what I had fantasized? It didn't seem likely.

Mitch came bouncing back. "I know these are probably huge for you," he handed me a pair of high top sneakers, "But as they're high top, they'll probably stay on. And I've got two pair of sox there."

"So I see." I sat on the edge of the car seat and pulled on the two pair of sox he handed me, and the high top sneakers.

"Let me tie them," Mitch said, kneeling on the ground and tightening the laces, then tying them snugly. "How's that?"

"Not bad, really. Well, I must look particularly gorgeous now, I hope you're serious about showing me something, and that you're not just trying to make some kind of idiot out of me."

"No, no. No kind of idiot. Come with me and watch your footing." Mitch turned on a high-intensity flashlight and pointed it at the ground. Taking my hand, he led me forward, then suddenly, he completely disappeared into the ground. I extricated my hand and backed away.

"Come on, follow me," he urged.

Chapter XI
Mitch's Big Secret

"Where are you, I mean, what's there?"

"There're steps." He shined the light up the steps from where he'd seemed to disappear. "Do you see them?"

"Just barely. But how weird. Why are there steps into the earth?" I made a great leap of trust as I took the first step down, very, very cautiously. It seemed fairly solid. A step carved out of the earth.

"Come on, keep coming, that's right now, take another step."

I took the next three steps, then turned around and looked up. A few stars peeked through the buttermilk clouds nearly covering the night sky. I took another step down, and the sky disappeared behind the ceiling of earth.

"Where is this?" I looked around, and what I could make out in the faint glow of Mitch's flashlight were walls, a sidewalk, and what looked like an ancient billboard.

"This is a part of Seattle's underground city. Have you heard of it?"

"Yes. My dad was talking about it, he wanted to go on some tour. But Mom and I thought it sounded funky. I mean, we couldn't believe that there'd be much to see. But this is amazing."

"This is a part of the underground city that's cut off from the section that's on the tour."

"How did you find out about it?"

"I like to discover things no one knows, so whenever I can get away from my uncle, I go exploring. I had gone on the underground city tour with my dad years ago when I was eleven, and I never could stop thinking about it. It seemed obvious to me that there'd be more underground city somewhere adjacent to the part that one can see on the tour. So I studied city maps.

"Then I went to the library and a librarian helped me dig out an old, old map, and I figured out where it would be likely that there'd be more of the underground city. Then I just kept poking around until I found a sort of gigantic rabbit hole and just took it from there."

"You mean, you dug it out?" I asked, completely incredulous.

"Yes. I dug it out. I keep hoping no one else will stumble on my discovery. If kids stumble on it, they'll certainly vandalize it, and if adults come upon it, they'll figure out a way to make money with it—make another tour of it or add it to the present tour—or something."

I sat on one of the steps, listening to Mitch and trying to take in everything that surrounded me. "But ... first of all, I don't understand why there's an underground city."

"In 1889, there was a terrible fire and something like thirty-two blocks of downtown Seattle burned down. Think about it. It must have been unbelievably awful. But the people didn't let it stop them. That's the part I like." He came over and sat on the step below me.

"Seattle already had this problem with the fact that a lot of downtown had been built below sea level, so when the tide came in, the water backed up into the toilets and water flushed into the bathroom instead of out of it. So the people said at that time, 'this fire has been a good thing, we'll build a new city on top of the old one, and we'll get rid of that pesky plumbing problem.'"

He stopped talking and studied me for a moment. "Well," he stood up, "are you going to come the rest of the way down, or stay perched up there?"

"I'm coming the rest of the way down." I stood and continued on down the steps and onto the wooden planks of the underground sidewalk. "This is all so amazing. And unbelievable, and yet, here I am!" I felt again a bit nervous about his remarkable intelligence and maturity. How could I possibly be interesting and intelligent enough for him?

When I came up beside him, Mitch trained the light of his flashlight on the billboard. "Millie's Millinery," it said over a faint sepia drawing of a Victorian woman wearing a huge, billowing hat. Curiously, she appeared to be looking right up the stairs at the night stars.

"She's beautiful," I whispered.

"Isn't she?" We stood reverently contemplating Miss Millie from a bygone era for a few moments, then Mitch took my hand and we silently headed down the sidewalk. We came to the front porch of a house, and he took me up onto it.

"I've been thinking about bringing a chair or something to put on the porch here, but it'd have to be a real antique from the time before the fire. I saw a wicker sort of fainting couch in an antique store, but it's way too expensive." He led me through the front door into the house. "All that's left of the house is this foyer and the living room, but isn't the wood-work fabulous? Even after all these years, and in this humid environment, it's still perfectly good."

I peered around at the scrollwork of the dark wooden Victorian doorways and archways and window moldings, the scent of wood and earth mingling into a musty, lonely aroma. "It's fabulous. I don't understand how it's still in such fantastic condition."

Mitch nodded. "I know. I don't understand it either. Sometimes I think it's a pity to let that beautiful woodwork rot and go to waste, and sometimes I feel that's exactly what it should do, to pass on in time in the house it's a part of. Should we sit on the porch?"

"Okay." I felt oddly out of time and even kind of out of body. The heavy presence of that other time in this undisturbed place seemed to quietly steal into me. I felt like I wasn't exactly myself. A bit dazed and overwhelmed, I followed Mitch back onto the porch and sat on the steps. "I suppose it's always dark here."

"Pretty much. But light filters down on a sunny day, and if you stay for a while with the flashlight turned off, your eyes adjust. You can make things out surprisingly clearly after a while. There is some phosphorescence in the walls that adds a hazy light. You can begin to imagine what it was like to have lived here. The city takes on a kind of life, like in a dream."

Mitch had been standing over me, gesturing down the sidewalk into the darkness, but now he came and sat behind me, putting his arms around my shoulders and held me close, without saying a word. I suddenly became aware of why Dad was so concerned about Mitch. Without even trying to get me to do anything like some silly boys tried to do, Mitch had taken me to a place down deep in myself where, if he asked more of me, I had no idea if I'd be able to say no.

But he didn't. I could sense he wanted my friendship more than anything. But, at the same time, I was not averse to sharing a first kiss. As if I'd said something out loud, Mitch leaned down and gently kissed my cheek, my lips.

Could any moment be more perfect, I wondered as I fell into the maelstrom of his warm fragrance. I leaned into him, and experienced the strangest sensation of familiarity, as if I had been here, in the safety and strength of his arms many, many times before, while at the same time, the thrill of his embrace was entirely new.

I felt I could have stayed there forever. I felt as if this was where I was meant to be, as if all my life had been about coming to this moment. I heard

Mitch's heart beating, I felt my pulse racing. I knew I would lock away this moment forever, for the rest of my life.

I also knew that I had better pull away because all of these thoughts and feelings were more than I could handle at the moment. It was as if I had telegraphed my thought as Mitch, ever so slightly, ever so gently pulled back from me and gazed into my eyes.

"Your eyes, dear Nikki, I will never be able to leave them, as long as you will let me be a part of your life."

Overwhelmed, on the verge of tears I didn't understand, I nodded, and moved out of his embrace. Not because I wanted to, but because, at that moment I had to.

"I ... I cannot imagine anything that would make me not want to have you in my life." I looked over at Millie, gazing up at the stars, forever and forever. "But I've never felt like this before. I've never had any experience like this. At all. In any way. So I don't ... I don't ...."

Mitch reached out and took my hand, stood beside me and looked at Millie too. "I understand what you're trying to say, Nikki. I know I'm a bit older than you, but it's the same for me. Or maybe even more so. I've been completely sheltered, not even in public school. Not even with a friend of any sort. Not even a guy to climb trees with."

He leaned his cheek against my hair. "I guess we're in the same little raft, more or less."

"Yes," I agreed. "The same little raft on a calm lake."

"I'd better be getting you back home."

"Um," I nodded, reluctant to change anything, reluctant to leave. I looked back over my shoulder into the depths of the quiet, vintage Seattle, sleeping peacefully here underground with her dreams of memories. "I suppose you're right."

Even as I said the words, a dark feeling stole over me. Something was waiting in my near future to disturb this perfect happiness. But if I never left this spot, it—whatever "it" was—could not reach me.

Still holding my hand, Mitch led me to the earthen stairs that Millie watched over, and I followed, trying to set aside the unclear-yet-unpleasant premonition.

But the foreboding grew with each step. I kept it to myself and resolved to protect the precious feelings of being with Mitch, safe, familiar and exciting, all at once.

When we emerged back into the night from our subterranean exploration, the clouds had gathered into a solid mass, and a delicate rain began to fall. By the time we got home, a deluge opened up the sky that we could hardly see through.

"I'm glad you don't have to drive somewhere else to get home now," I said as he drove into the parking structure. I'd pulled off the sweats, high tops, and sox on the way home. I slipped on my pumps.

"It's nice to be home, both of us at the same time."

He took my hand and kissed my fingers, looking into my eyes. Then he leaned over and whispered, "one wonders, when one imagines the future, what it would be like to always come home together."

He pulled back from me as if afraid he'd said too much and looked out the windshield, where there was nothing but a cinder block wall.

Changing the mood completely he said, "You know what? I'm starving. I forgot about eating. Shall we brave the elements and find something?"

"Let's just go up and order a pizza," I suggested. I felt quiet and private.

"That sounds like a very cozy plan," Mitch agreed.

"Then let's do it!"

We ran around the building, giggling, and dashing through the door, thanking the Homer-clone who let us in. My heart raced the elevator to the seventh floor—I felt so elated with Mitch, while still being troubled by the foreboding sensation that had not abated. The elevator doors shushed open and we tip-toed down the hall. I unlocked the door and let us in.

All was still and quiet.

In fact, the rooms were strangely silent. I could tell my parents were not there. I looked around for a note, but no note. I went down the hall to their room, pushed the door open a crack—no one was there, although the pink sweatsuit Mom had on earlier was thrown across the bed and the closet door was partly open, which was very unusual for them, even when they were in a hurry.

I came back into the living room. "Something's strange. Like they left in a hurry."

"Are you worried?"

"Ahm, yes."

"Do you want me to leave?"

"No. Oh, please, no. I want you here, of course. Let's order that pizza. I suppose they just went out to get some ice cream or some-such. Anyway," I said, more for myself than Mitch, "they didn't expect me back until eleven, so they'll be back by then. Let's take advantage of the privacy and order that pizza so we can have it all to ourselves, *he, he.*"

"Diabolical plan," Mitch agreed, getting out his phone.

Twenty minutes later we were elbow deep in hot, fresh pizza.

I couldn't help myself, I looked at Mitch wondering, did he know he was so beautiful? Didn't he know he could be with the most beautiful girl he could find?

"What are you thinking so loudly that I can't eat?" he finally asked.

"Oh, sorry. Well, I'm, ahm, like, that is, you know ....."

"Can't know if you don't tell me."

"I'm thinking, you could have the most beautiful girl you could find." An image of Stephanie popped into my mind. An unbidden and depressing picture. The two of them would look fantastic together. "And you're so incredibly intelligent."

"You're beautiful, Nikki. But that's not what's most important. I like who you are, the way you express your emotions, the way you smell, the way you look, I mean, your facial expressions. They're very endearing. I like everything about you.

"I've found that, for myself, what other people call beautiful is often sort of boring, while someone who is open and curious, with a kind of innocence

... that's beautiful to me. You are my definition of beautiful. And as far as intelligence goes, well, my dear friend, you can certainly hold your own."

"Thanks," I said feeling both happy and self-conscious. I wasn't used to getting such a barrage of compliments. "I don't know if I feel confident enough to accept it, but I appreciate it."

I finished my half-eaten slice of pizza before asking a daring question. "But don't you know you have that kind of perfect beauty? Straight nose, full lips, huge, beautiful eyes, incredible skin, lean body. Would you say your beauty is boring?"

"Yes, I would, if I look like you say. I'd love to have a nose that has some character, with a bump in it, or something."

"You could break it," I teased.

"I could. But my uncle has broken his nose half-a-dozen times in his life, and all a broken nose does for you is make it hard to breathe, and hard to smell smells. I don't want that either. I hope the way I look isn't boring to you."

"Oh, no! Not in any way, not in the least." How could he even say such a thing?

Right then, I heard a key in the front door. Mom and Dad came into the living room, wet and looking anxious. I was frightened by their twin looks of anxiety—I'd never seen quite that expression before. And I knew that they were about to put meaning to the dark premonition that had poked at me all evening.

Chapter XII
Crisis!

"What's wrong?" I perched on the edge of the sofa, not wanting to hear what they were going to say.

"We've just come from the police station," Mom said.

"They have most of the rest of the furniture and paintings," Dad went on. "We had to go down to identify them. And, apparently, the antique dealer was able to identify the person who sold the things to him."

Mitch stood up. I saw he was trembling. "My uncle."

"Yes," Mom said. "They're on their way now to arrest him."

Mitch moved toward the door.

"It won't serve to try to warn him, son. Isn't it better to let justice take its course?" Dad said.

"I'm not going to warn him. I can't wait to see them cart him off. But my mother will need me. Excuse me, please," he passed by Mom and Dad. I found myself hoping Dad would grab him, not let him go. But he didn't and Mitch disappeared quietly through the door, closing it firmly behind him.

I looked from Mom to Dad, hoping one of them would start to laugh, and say it was all a joke, that they'd planned it with Mitch. Hoping that he'd come back through the door with a big grin on his face. But I saw in both their faces that it was just as real and awful as it seemed. I could see they felt terrible. But I couldn't accept that my perfect evening had come to this horrible end.

"Don't worry Sweetie," Dad said, 'Mitch will be okay, I'm sure."

"But what do you think of him, if he's the nephew of a criminal?"

"I think that I'm a pretty good judge of moral character, and Mitch has good moral character. I'm not going to judge him rashly because of something someone else did—even if it is his uncle. And I'm sure he'll need all the support and understanding we can provide."

At that moment, there was the muffled sound of several people moving down the hall, then a terrifying pounding on the neighboring door. We all held our breath as we listened to the tones of conversation without being able to make out any words—a conversation that became heated, then very quiet. Then there was the muffled sound of several bodies moving back down the hall to the elevator.

And that was all.

"It'll be okay," Dad reassured, coming over and putting his arm around my shoulder.s "Don't cry."

I reached up and brushed at my eyes and only then realized I was crying. "But we had such a perfect evening. And we even came back early and ordered pizza, and we were having so much fun. Why did this have to happen right now, tonight?"

"Better sooner than letting Mitch's uncle think he can get away with it, don't you think?"

"Maybe."

"I'm wiped out, but I'm all wound up, too," Mom said. "how about some hot chocolate?"

I nodded, but I didn't feel like having hot chocolate. In fact, the pizza wasn't sitting particularly well at the moment. But hanging out with my folks in the kitchen was at least comforting.

While we sipped our hot chocolate, and Mom and Dad gave me more details of their trip to the police station, I found my attention wandering. Why didn't Mitch call and tell me what had happened? So what if it was late, I wanted him to reassure me that he was all right, that everything was all right. That he meant what he said to me tonight ... before everything fell apart.

How was he? My thoughts went around and around in a worried circle.

"It seems he might have called and let us know how things went," Mom said, speaking my thoughts.

"He may be embarrassed," Dad suggested. "It's possible we won't see him for a while."

That brought me out of my introspection. Dad was right. Mitch was proud—I didn't know much about him yet, but I did know that. "Do you think he won't want to see me?"

"Oh, Pumpkin Pie, I'm sure he'll want to see you, but he may be too embarrassed for awhile. Be patient—let him figure it out in his own way, in his own time. I mean, as long as it all comes out right in the end, that's all that matters. Your Mom and I certainly don't bear him any grudge. But you have to admit, it's not a usual situation."

"Well, I should hope not," Mom nodded emphatically. "Neighbors robbing you blind. There'd be no society if that were usual."

Obviously, Mom did not share Dad's complete coolness with the situation. She was angry. There was a good chance she'd say something to Mitch if he did come by before she got over it.

I went from wishing with all my heart that Mitch would call or stop by, to hoping with all my might that he wouldn't for a few days until things settled. As long as everyone kept saying Mitch couldn't be held responsible for something he didn't know about, I believed it'd eventually be okay. And I'd be okay with Mom being all weird if she wanted to hold him responsible in some way—as long as she kept it to herself.

*   *

I got my wish. For days I didn't see or hear sight or sound of anyone in the neighboring apartment. Dad asked if we'd seen or heard Mitch or his mother. Mom and I shook our heads.

Then Dad knocked me for a loop by saying, "Maybe they've moved."

My heart sank. It was a possibility. "But if they were living here rent-free," I argued, "could they leave?"

Dad gave me a studied look, like, when did you get so smart? "You make an excellent point. If they're there, they sure know how to lie low. And if they moved, they could hardly take anything down this hall without us being aware of it. They might have gone to stay with someone, though. Until the dust settles."

"Days go by without seeing most of our neighbors, and we don't think anything of that," I said.

"True," Dad agreed. "So they're probably still there, you're right."

The idea of Mitch having moved without even saying good-bye stuck in me like a painful sliver. Could he do that? Would he? What if I never saw him again? Why didn't I just go knock on his door? Why was that so hard for me? One reason was because I had called him and texted him several times, and he did not answer. Anyway, never mind the phone. I wanted to see him!

The next day I was so miserable, I decided I had to take action. I knew what I had to do. After school, I didn't even stop at my apartment. I went straight to his door and knocked. It took every ounce of my courage. I stood in front of the peephole so that, if anyone was there, they'd know exactly who was on the other side of the door.

No one answered, but I heard a faint stirring inside. I waited a full minute, then knocked again. And stood my ground.

Finally, the door opened a crack, with the chain on. It was dark on the other side of the door, and I could not make out anyone.

"What do you want, little neighbor girl?" a woman's voice asked. It was thick with the accent I loved about Mitch's voice, although his was much less pronounced. The sound caught in my heart.

"I want to talk with Mitch."

"He is not here."

"Where is he?"

"I don't know. He has been gone for days."

"You don't know? Aren't you worried about him?"

"He can take care of himself. He knows what he's doing. He's at a ... what's it called, crossroads. It's his journey. He's in God's hands."

"Well, I'm worried about him." I have no idea what made me so strong that I could carry on this confrontational conversation with his mother. But I was strong.

"Then you should go find him. If you are meant to find him, you will." With that, she firmly shut and locked the door.

I stood there disappointed and confused for a few moments. Then I realized that of course, I knew where he was. I just had no idea how to get there.

I walked slowly back to my apartment, trying to sort out how to make the next move. Inside, the place was very quiet. Mom left a note on the entryway table.

"Getting some groceries. Be back soon."

Something came over me that I had never felt before. I opened the drawer and pulled out the extra set of Mom's car's keys. I dug in my wallet to make sure I had my learner's permit I got in the summer just before we moved here and that I had almost never used. It was better than nothing.

I slipped out the door and crept down the hall to the stairs, then flew down the seven flights of stairs. The stairs came out beside the elevators, and beside the doorway from the stairs was a back door to the parking structure. Just a quick turn out one door and through the other—I prayed that Homer was facing the street.

At the bottom of the stairs, I paused, caught my breath. If Homer saw me, I waited to gather my calm, it'd be enough to have to explain why I took the stairs. Just exercising, Homer.

I opened the door, stepped out. Homer had his back to me talking to the tiny woman with the yappy dog I'd seen—and heard—every now and then. He was trying to be heard over the dog's shrill noise.

I stepped through the back door, ran into the parking structure, fumbled with the keys, dropped them. Picked them up. Got in the car, started it and then asked my self, "What do you think you're doing, Nikki?"

But I didn't have time to answer. I had to move, or I would lose courage. Or whatever this weird emotion was that made me suddenly act completely out of character.

I had never, ever, ever done anything even remotely like this in my life. When I was a little girl, a friend of mine said she was going to run away from home. She'd packed a little suitcase and everything. I couldn't imagine how she could even think of doing such a thing. I asked her where she would go, what she was going to eat, where she would sleep, what her parents would think, they would be so worried.

And now I'd basically stolen my mother's car and didn't even leave her a note. Oh—I had really become crazy!

I was glad it wasn't dark yet so I could get my bearings. I tried to remember exactly the route Mitch had driven when he took me to his underground hideaway. We'd started from the theatre about half-a-mile away. So I went to the theatre, and then worked out the same initial turns he took. I remembered that he then went quite a distance on a road that wasn't very busy. So I followed what I thought he'd done.

About twenty minutes later, I saw familiar terrain, as the sun made its way below the western horizon. And there it was! The grassy knoll where'd he'd taken me that night, now seeming ever so long ago. I stopped the engine and gripped the steering wheel. Courage, Nikki, I told myself. You've come this far, don't wimp out now!

I got the flashlight and started to prowl around in the fast-falling darkness. The place looked completely abandoned. I felt spooky. I knew I ought to text Mom, who was surely becoming alarmed. But I dared not stop. I had to find that rabbit hole in the earth before darkness fell completely. A loamy, earthy scent rose up from the damp ground, and a cool breeze buffeted around me. I felt as if I didn't exist at all.

Then I almost fell into the hole before I saw it. I went down a couple of steps carefully. It didn't feel as though anyone was there, other than the two-dimensional Millie, on the billboard, eternally, gazing skyward.

I continued to the bottom of the stairs, the musty aroma rising up around me, then I walked cautiously on the wooden sidewalk, the beam of my flashlight barely giving me enough light to see my next step. When I came to the house where Mitch and I had sat on the porch before, I went up the steps, then peered around in the foyer. No Mitch. I began to wonder how I could have been so wrong about where he was. I knew I ought to turn around and hurry home.

But I couldn't resist continuing, now that I was here. I followed the wooden sidewalk further into the underground Victorian Seattle, without any idea of how far the sidewalk might continue, without any idea if it was safe to walk on these ancient, damp planks. The sidewalk continued on, fading into an impenetrable darkness.

I passed a part of another house, and that was when I decided I really must turn back. That was also when I heard the soft-footed step of someone in the near distance. Fright ran through me like electricity.

What if there was someone I didn't know down here? It was entirely possible. Just because Mitch discovered this place didn't mean others hadn't.

I tried desperately to hold my breath and to make myself invisible, shrinking up against the wall of the house. How strange and unreal the whole situation! If anything happened to me, no one would ever find me until they discovered Mom's car—if even then.

Whoever was walking on the sidewalk in the darkness was very nearly upon me. The strong beam of a high-powered flashlight played on the wooden sidewalk. The person walked at a slow, thoughtful pace, obviously not looking for young women to pounce upon. I honestly wanted to shriek like every high school girl in every horror movie. But I kept my silence, my heart pounding.

And then—I made out Mitch's face in the faint, shadowed light, and the breath flowed from me audibly.

It was Mitch's turn to be scared out of his wits—clearly not expecting any girl to pounce upon him. "What the ... who is that?" He flashed the light in my eyes. "Dominique? What are you doing here?"

"Shopping for oranges," I answered in a sudden fit of silly.

Mitch heaved a huge sigh. I couldn't tell if it was a recouping equilibrium sigh, or a sigh of depression. "No oranges down here this time of year." He walked up to me but kept an uncomfortable distance between us.

"I can't believe you're here." He seemed angry, and after the intense emotions I'd been going through all day, I was afraid I was dangerously close to bursting into tears.

"I'm here," I answered in a little, quavery voice.

"Well, come on, let's sit on the porch."

We sat on the bottom step, Mitch still staying a couple of feet away. "Now tell me—why are you here?"

"I haven't seen you in days. You don't answer your phone, you don't answer my texts. I don't know why you're hiding from me. I'm not angry with you, my parents aren't angry with you. I know a lot has happened, and I can understand you need to spend some time alone. But don't you know I'm going crazy not hearing anything, not knowing anything about you?"

Mitch shook his head, studying the wooden planks beneath his feet. "I don't know what I thought, or what I thought you thought. I've just been trying to make my guilt go away. My mother needs me too, but I just can't stay in that place right now. There's so much you don't know, that I don't want you to know. Please, please—let it alone. Let's at least keep the memory of that one perfect evening.

"My uncle, my family, my heritage are going to haunt me. I can't get away from it. I can't have a future apart from them, I can't have a future that's moral and good. Crime is my birthright."

"What incredible nonsense." I moved closer to Mitch and took his hand. "You can be anything you want, you can do anything you want. I know you're good. You're not responsible for what your uncle did—no one holds you responsible for what he did. You didn't know your uncle committed a crime, so stop feeling guilty."

"You're wrong."

"What do you mean?" I felt my heart sink ... I was about to hear something that would cause me worse pain yet.

"Please, Nikki, do not insist."

"Well, I do insist, if it's something that's coming between us, you have to tell me."

"I *did* know what my uncle had done. He's been talking about hitting your apartment for months. He was going to do the job while the place was vacant. He didn't know it'd been sublet, and he'd planned to do the job the first week you folks moved in.

"You see now what I'm trying to deal with? I knew he was going to rob you, and I didn't do anything. I did return your ring, though. Boy, I thought he was going to come unhinged when he couldn't find it, but I just couldn't let him keep it when it meant so much to you."

I felt my whole body tighten. Now I understood what Mom meant when she said she felt violated by the robbery. Here was this person who pretended to be interested in me, who pretended to be my friend. But he wasn't. He was an accomplice to a crime.

Suddenly I was standing, although I didn't know I'd moved, and my whole body trembled. "You knew and you didn't do anything to stop it? How could you pretend to be a friend while knowing who had committed this horrible, invasive, crime?

"I thought you liked us, I thought you cared about me. Never mind me, I thought you respected my parents. But I guess you must really hate us, you must be jealous, because we're a real family, and all you have is some abusive uncle you can't get away from. That is, until the police came and took him away."

I moved away from the porch. "I can't believe it. Everything else I could handle, the robbery, the fact that it was your uncle who robbed us, that fact that you disappear and don't even give me a call—all that I could take. But the idea of you laughing at us, when you're an accomplice to a crime, it's too much. Shame on you! Really, shame on you!"

I burst into tears, blinded with the pain of being so wrong about Mitch. Was I going to stay stupid all my life, or did I just have to stay away from getting close to anyone?

I stumbled back up the sidewalk to the steps and climbed them as fast as I could, blinded by my tears, nearly tripping, finally gaining the outside world, now truly dark with night.

I got in the car and pulled onto the road, trying to see through my tears, pain, and anger. I knew that was dangerous behind the wheel, and not only that, I could soon get lost.

I pulled into the first gas station I came to and got out my phone. I started a text to Mom, but I just couldn't think, couldn't decide what to say. I couldn't say I was on my way home, because I didn't want to be around them right now.

But I had to talk with someone. I felt I was about to explode. Then Alex popped into my mind. We'd become bantering, teasing pals at school, but maybe I could talk with him. I dialed his number.

"Hey, Nikki," he said, all happy-sounding.

"Hi, Alex."

"What's wrong?"

"Is it that obvious?"

"Yes."

"I ... I just need to talk with someone."

"Well, come on over to the store and we'll talk."

"But, the store's closed."

"Guess what? I have a key. And I'll have tea and cheesecake waiting for you."

How wonderful was Alex? "But ... I'm not at home. I'm ... I don't exactly know where I am, but it'll be a while before I can get there."

"Strange. Where do you think you are?"

I told him the name of the street I was on, and the gas station I was at.

"Oh! You're right, that's not close. What are you doing there? Never mind, we'll talk when you get here. Come to the back and ring the buzzer."

Then he told me a simple route to get back to territory I was familiar with. Twenty minutes later, I saw the "Zingas' Grocery" sign with huge relief, parked on the street, went around to the back and pressed the buzzer.

Alex let me in. Without a word, he led me to a little table, where waited a steaming pot of tea and a huge slice of cheesecake. He'd only turned on a small light, and it all looked so cozy.

I sat. Alex poured me a cup of tea. "What's up?"

"Well ...."

"Wait. First, do your folks know you're here?"

"No."

"Call them."

"Right." I got out my phone and texted Mom's phone. "Home soon. Don't worry." I shut off my phone then looked across the table at Alex. He was completely attentive. No goofy little boy now, but a real, listening, good friend.

"Thank you for ... this, for talking to me. I just didn't know who else to turn to. I can't talk about this with my parents."

Alex nodded, but didn't say anything.

"Since our place was robbed, I really haven't been too upset about it. I don't know if you know this part, but the other night the police learned who did it, and it was our neighbor. It was Mitch's—my neighbor?—his uncle. I was okay with that, because I thought, you know, that Mitch couldn't help what his uncle did. But then he disappeared."

"Who disappeared?"

"Mitch. My neighbor. The boy next door. Anyway, I haven't seen him or heard from him since the police came and arrested his uncle. And I couldn't stand it anymore. I mean, I had to talk to him. I had to tell him that I didn't hold him responsible for what his uncle did.

"Then I ... I found him, and I told him I couldn't be mad at him or hold him responsible for something he didn't know about. I said that if he'd known his uncle was going to rob us, he would have told someone, so it wouldn't happen.

"Then he ..." Much to my chagrin, I burst into tears. "He told me he had known about it. That his uncle had planned to rip our apartment off for months, before we even moved in. He'd intended to do it when the place was vacant. Instead, he did it when we went away for the weekend."

"That's too bad," Alex said. "You must feel like you've been betrayed."

"Yes! Betrayed." I wished I could stop sobbing, but I just couldn't. "I mean, Mitch and I went to a movie last weekend, and then he took me to a hiding place of his and I thought we were so close, I thought we were sharing something beautiful and honest. But he was making a fool of me and my parents. That's the part that makes me so angry. My dad was even going to help him get into college. No wonder he said his education was unorthodox. I guess being trained how to rob your neighbors blind and make them love you in the bargain is an unorthodox education, all right.

"And he acted so sweet. Really, he's an incredible actor, saying he admired my family so much and wished he could be in a family like ours. But I think he was jealous and petty, and probably really hates us."

"Hmm." Alex said quietly. "You truly believe he hates you?"

"Well, maybe not hate, exactly. But I think he wanted to hurt us because we have each other. He told me that he returned my grandmother's ring to me. He snuck it away from his uncle and put it back in my jewelry box, like that's supposed to make all the difference."

"He brought back your grandmother's ring? When did he do that?"

"The day after we came back from our weekend at the beach."

"How would he do that? Wasn't someone home then?"

"I don't know how he did it. I suppose my Mom went out and did some shopping, I suppose he did it then."

"Are you saying he has free access to your apartment?"

"So it would seem. I mean, they ripped us off without any sign of breaking and entering. That's what the police were so mystified about. Eugh! I didn't think about that. He has some kind of access to our apartment, doesn't he?"

"Looks like. Had you told him how much your grandmother's ring means to you?"

"Well, ahm ... no! That's right, how would he even know it was my ring, or what it meant to me? There's something very weird going on."

"There are some unanswered questions. But let's look at it. Yes, my Dad has some problems with Mitch's family. But I know Mitch a little bit. I've chatted with him a few times here in the store. He always asks me about school.

"Anyway, he seems to have quite a lot going for him. I'm not saying it's not possible that, under his veneer, he's conniving and immoral. But it doesn't fit with him taking you out on a date and returning your ring. If he hated your family and if he was supportive of his uncle's heist ... well, it just doesn't fit together.

"He's still a minor, and he's living in his uncle's home. His uncle really is kinda scary. Mitch may be frightened of him, especially if he feels he needs to protect his mother. And if that's the case, he may have felt that he needed to protect his mother and also try to protect your family, too.

"But what if doing the one sacrificed doing the other? He'd choose his mother over a few items being taken from your apartment, don't you think? Plus, he returned something to you that would be worth a lot of money to him. If he didn't care about you, he would surely not return a small, easy to liquidate, valuable item."

Alex poured me some more tea, as I'd pretty much gulped the whole cup down—it made me feel so much more calm. Well, the tea and Alex's soothing, logical voice.

"Tough spot to be in," he went on. "I can understand his dilemma. But the biggest curiosity is, how did he know the ring was yours, and how did he know it has such tremendous personal significance to you, if you didn't tell him? And how did he return it without anyone knowing he did? I'd think you'd want those questions answered. Even if he is terrible, I wouldn't want to alienate him until I knew more. Because it's decidedly all very odd."

"Wow, Alex, wow, you're amazing! And you're absolutely right. Thank you so much!"

"You're welcome, my friend. Finish your cheesecake and get home. It's a school night, young lady," he said in a mocking tone, but sounding uncannily like my dad.

"You sounded just like my dad!"

"One of my many talents."

I wolfed down the rest of the cheesecake, stood up, gave Alex a hug and hurried out to the car. When I drove into the parking structure, Homer, standing outside, saw me and pointed at me like, "there-you-are-thank-God-you're-alive-and-are-you-in-trouble!"

So when I flew through the front door I said, "Yes, I'm alive and I know, I'm in deep."

Chapter XIII
Mystery!

When I walked into the apartment, Mom and Dad were on the sofa, alarm printed on both their faces.

"I'm sorry," I said before either of them spoke.

"Sorry doesn't cut it, Dominique," Dad said. "What is going on?"

"So much has happened. Mitch never talked to me. He never answered his phone when I called, or my texts. I went and talked to his mother after school today and she said she hadn't seen him for days, and didn't know where he was. And I just kinda freaked out. She said if I was meant to find him I would find him.

"I had an idea where he was and I went there. I mean, I just couldn't stop myself, I went there. And he was there ...."

I'd spouted all this without a pause, standing in the doorway, the awful feeling crawling up inside me again, the calmness Alex had produced completely gone.

Mom, who had said nothing, came over to me, wrapped her arms around me and pulled me to the sofa. She hugged me and said, very softly, "You scared me to death, Nikki."

I nodded into her sweater. I'd never seen Mom so scared that she was quiet. Right now, Mom and Dad had reversed their roles, with Dad ranting and Mom quiet. I saw the protector in Dad, and real, true fear in Mom. I resolved never, ever to make them feel like that again.

"I know, Mom. What I had to do was right, but the way I did it was wrong. I feel so many kinds of horrible and crummy and depressed."

"We'll talk about your punishment later, but right now tell us where you've been."

"Okay. So Mitch's mother said if I was meant to find him, I'd find him. And I did. I told him he didn't have to hide from me because I wasn't angry with him. He couldn't help something he didn't know about.

"But then ... then he told me that he had known his uncle was going to rob our place. He'd intended to do it when it was vacant before we moved in. Then when we moved in, we messed up his plans.

"When Mitch told me that, I became so furious. How could he possibly know his uncle intended to rob us and not do anything about it? How could he be so friendly with all of us, knowing his uncle's plan? I ran away from him. I couldn't bear how miserable I felt. And I wanted to talk with someone my age. I just ... that's what I felt I had to do. So I called Alex ...."

"Who's Alex?" Dad said, all stormy again.

"Mr. Zingas' son. We're in World Lit together, and we're sort of pals. We weren't close, but, still, he's my closest pal here. And he met me at the store and made me some tea and talked with me. He is really remarkable." I heaved the biggest sigh I think I've ever breathed in my life. "And then I came home."

"And then you came home," Dad repeated, incredulous.

"I know. If I'm grounded for life, so be it. I don't have anything going on anyway, so it won't be different from life as usual."

"What did this Alex say that was so remarkable?" Dad asked.

"First, he really listened to everything I said, and then he said something like, Mitch was torn between his new feelings of loyalty to us, while having to worry about his mother. He said he's met Mitch's uncle and he's really scary. He said that if he were in Mitch's shoes, he'd be in a dilemma, wanting to do right by us and having to take care of his mother. He said that the fact that Mitch returned my ring means a lot about his trying to stand by his morals."

"Returned your ring?" Mom asked, amazed.

"Oh, yeah. I left that out. Mitch told me he returned my ring because it means so much to me."

"But I found it in your jewelry box."

"I know, Mom. But even when you handed it to me, I knew it hadn't been in my jewelry box. It was missing the night we got back from the coast. But it was pointless to argue with you about it."

"Did you ask Mitch if he returned it?"

"I didn't have to. He told me he returned it. Then Alex asked if I'd told Mitch about how important Grammy's ring is to me, and I said no. And he pointed out that that was pretty strange. And he's right. So it seems like they have access to our place...."

"I had the locks changed the next day," Mom said. "I didn't leave the apartment until the locks were re-keyed. I tried the old keys myself, and they didn't work."

"I know," I said.

"Well, that gives me the creeps." Mom shivered involuntarily.

"I don't know the answer to all the questions," I went on. "But I want to find out. Alex thought it'd be smarter to try and find out the answers before entirely cutting off all ties with Mitch."

"There is something really fishy here," Dad said, a deep frown growing from his forehead to his whole face. "I'm not about to have my family at risk. I think we ought to go house hunting tomorrow.

"This is a beautiful place and we'll never find anything like it for the same rent, but safety is more important. If your very neighbors pose a threat, well, there's not much one can do about that other than move away from them. That's why I was so pleased with Homer and the other doormen and the security guards here. But they're seven floors away."

"Oh!" Mom sighed, glancing at the piano.

"Well, Dad, I don't think we're in any kind of danger now. Mitch's uncle is in jail, and he was the threat. Let's see if we can find out more first. It would really mess up everything, including your work if we had to move again."

"It'll mess up my work if I have to worry about you two all day every day if this place isn't safe."

"Nikki's right, Sweetheart. Let's not go off in a tangent. With Mitch's uncle put away, and Homer on hyper-vigilant, we're probably safer here now than anywhere."

Wow! I was impressed with Mom's logic. It was really interesting to see my parents switch roles.

"I think Alex was right—that Mitch was painted into a corner, and he didn't know which way to turn. Rather than just running away, I'd like to know more," I added.

"And I'd certainly like to know more," Mom agreed. She gave me a long, studied look. I could see she was sorting out some decision. I braced myself for the worst. "You went to a friend you've made, you were given very good advice, you've taken in that advice, and you feel happier," she said.

"Yes," I answered simply, wondering where she was going with this line of thinking.

"That's all I've ever wanted for you by having you go to therapists. Although the way you did what you did this evening is unacceptable, I am no longer going to make therapy appointments for you. From now on, you are welcome to make your own appointments with a counselor if you want, but you are too grown up for me to be making that decision for you. You've shown that you are resourceful by going to a peer, who helped you get a balanced perspective."

"Oh, Mom!" I couldn't say anything more.

"However, Nikki, if Mitch is part of the criminal element, I do not want you alone with him. And I agree with your dad, as much as I love this place, if in any way it continues to feel unsafe, we'll have to move."

Dad was nodding, nodding to everything Mom and I said to each other. "Okay," he said. "Let's sleep on it for tonight. Everything will seem clearer in the morning."

"Yeah, okay. I'm exhausted. I've never, ever had such an emotional roller-coaster day. And, again, I'm sorry for making you worry. I'll *never* do anything like this ever again." I kissed them good night and went to my room.

When I got there, I closed the door, closed the bathroom and closet doors, and turned the lights out. I lifted the leg of my brass bed, popped off the end cover, and felt Grammy's emerald tumble out into my hand. I crawled onto the bed and held the ring tightly. I could hear my parents carrying on a quiet but animated conversation in their room, every now and then I heard "Mitch" then "Nikki."

I wished my Grammy were here. She would see everything so clearly. Mom and Dad are awesome, but they're too close to the whole situation and too worried about me. It was wonderful to discover that Alex was so wise and smart. And he had inside knowledge of Mitch and his family.

But how could I determine if Mitch was a good guy in a bad environment or a bad guy who's very clever? Was he caught up in the middle of an awful situation and not sure himself which way he might turn? Could I help him? Or did he have to figure it out all by himself?

As I had these thoughts, addressing them to Grammy in my mind, the room fell very still, with a deep, deep, quiet. I couldn't hear my parents talking, I couldn't hear cars on the street below. Then I saw Grammy in front of me, much fainter than the previous time she'd appeared. In fact, I could only tell it was her more by the feeling than what I saw. I heard Grammy's voice in my head, not out loud in the room.

"My darling girl, I wish I could stay and help you through every problem you will ever have, but I can't. I can only tell you that if you follow your heart, it'll be the right thing to do. I'll not be able to come to you again, but you must know I'm with you, inside you, throughout this life. You have all the wisdom and patience I ever had. The best way for you to learn is to listen to the knowledge that flows through you and to follow the example of your parents. Your father is truly one of the gentlest, most moral men you'll ever meet. I was very privileged to be his mother."

I struggled to say something back to Grammy, but the syrupy feeling that had bathed me when I saw her before was now more like congealing tree sap. I could neither move nor speak, except deep in my mind, to simply meld with her.

I woke up the next morning, still fully clothed and still clutching Grammy's ring, knowing that I'd seen my grandmother for the last time. Strangely enough, I didn't cry. I felt a warmth of peace spread through me, and I understood that I was not sad that Grammy was farther away from me, because she needed to move forward on her journey.

"Yes, dearest Grammy, go. You're right, I'll figure it out, and I'll be okay. But I'll never stop loving you, and I'll probably never stop talking to you, and I'll never stop holding your ring to feel close to you. Thank you for pausing on your journey to give me comfort and advice."

I got out of bed and showered and dressed for school. It was going to be incredibly hard to concentrate on being a high school kid today, with all the adult things I had to sort out.

In the kitchen, Dad was alone, making waffles. "Good morning, Nikki. How did you sleep?"

"Pretty well, actually. Ahm, Dad, I'd like to tell you something, I mean, I think you'd like to know this, if you promise you won't think I'm crazy or something."

"I promise that even if I do think you're crazy, I won't let it affect my overall opinion of you too much."

"Funny. But I'm serious. Can you stop for a minute?"

Dad glanced over his shoulder at me. Something about my expression caught him, and made him realize I needed his undivided attention. "Okay, Sweetie, just let me pour this batter, and I'm all yours." He poured the batter into the waffle iron, then came over and sat in the breakfast booth across from me. He took my hand. "Is this about Mitch?"

"No. Well, sort of, I mean, it's because of Mitch that I ... Dad, I've seen Grandmother twice since we've lived here. On the night that the ring was stolen, and last night."

Dad gripped my hands a bit tighter, but he didn't say anything.

"What do you think of that, Dad?"

"I think my Mom was the strongest woman I've ever known, and it doesn't surprise me that she's got the power to come back and give you some attention. What did she say?"

"She said that she couldn't come to me again, but that it was all right because I had 'the wisdom' in me. And that I should follow the example of you and Mom, and that you are one of the gentlest, most moral men I'll ever know in my life, and she said it was a privilege to have been your mother."

Dad had shed a few tears at Grammy's funeral, but I'd never in my life seen Dad with tears streaming down his face like they were now. "Well, Angel-Girl," he finally said in a whisper, "I truly believe you saw her." He squeezed my hands then dried his face. "I don't know how to thank you for sharing that with me."

He stood and took the golden brown, fresh, fat, delicious smelling waffle from the waffle iron.

There was a peaceful quiet in the room between us. A couple minutes later Mom came in the kitchen. "It smells fantastic! Waffles from scratch—what inspired you?"

"Love and a raging appetite."

Mom nodded. "Orange juice, Nikki?"

"Okay."

"What have you decided about Mitch?" she asked as she poured three glasses of orange juice.

"That he has to figure out for himself if he's going to forgive himself and let me in his life, or not."

"Yes. That's good. Your dad and I have decided not to ground you, but you are not to go off alone with Mitch for the time being."

"Okay, Mom. That's more than fair. I'll be patient."

I thought it'd be almost impossible to be at school that day. But it wasn't. Knowing where Mitch was, shifting away from being furious at him and feeling betrayed by him, having gotten closer to Alex, and being in the after-glow of Grammy's visitation, all made me calm, centered and attentive to my school work.

But I did wonder when and how I'd get to talk to Mitch.

Chapter XIV
Oh Those Eyes!

As it turned out, I didn't have to wonder for long.

"Mitch called me," Mom said when I came through the door after school. "He said he's home now. He apologized to me. I was very moved by his sincerity. He wants you to call him."

My heart raced as I plopped my books down. It couldn't have been easy for him to gather up the courage to apologize to my mother. "What did he say?"

"He was clearly nervous. He stuttered. He said he knew he owed your dad and me an explanation and he hoped we'd give him a chance to talk with him."

"What did you say?"

"That we probably would. But I told him that he had to make things right with you first."

"Oh, Mom!" I couldn't say more. She was amazing!

"I see you're hurting, Nikki, and I don't want you to hurt if Mitch can make you feel better. Of course, he may not. But I know my Nikki will make the best of whatever happens."

I nodded and went to my room, then called him.

"Hi, Mitch, it's Nikki."

"Hi," he said quietly.

"Do you want to come over and talk? I mean, we have to talk in person. We can't have this conversation on the phone."

"With your folks and you, all at once?"

"No. Just me. We can talk in my room."

"Good. Because there's something else I didn't tell you."

"There's more?" What more could there possibly be?

"Sort of. Shall I come over now?"

"Please."

I hung up and looked around my room—not too bad, no underwear laying about, at least. The doorbell chimed, and I heard Mom answer it before I could get there.

"Hi," I said, coming down the hall. He turned and looked at me. *Ohh!* Those eyes! But I had to keep my head on straight, and I had to have a truthful conversation with him, whatever the results might be. "Mom, we're going into my room to talk, okay?"

"Okay. Leave the door open a bit."

"All right." Die of embarrassment, I thought. Right here, right now. Everyone knew what "leave the door open" meant.

"Make yourself comfortable," I said, closing the door as far as I dared while wishing I'd taken a chair into my room. All I had was the little backless boudoir chair and the bed.

Mitch looked around the room then sat on the floor.

I sat on the floor in front of him. "You said you have more things to tell me, and I have some things to say to you, so who starts?"

"I think you should begin," he answered. "Because part of what I have to say is, well, I have to show you something."

"Okay. When I talked with you yesterday—was it only yesterday?—I got so furious because you didn't do anything to stop your uncle from ripping us off. But then I talked with ... a bunch of people, and they all kind of said that since your uncle is an immoral, mean guy, and since you live with him and your mom, you might have been in an extremely tough spot, feeling responsible to take care of your mom, and at the same time maybe feeling terrible about what happened to us.

"Everyone reminded me that you could only do so much. And because of that, you were left with feeling guilty. And then I made it worse, I suppose by getting so angry with you."

Mitch nodded to everything I said. "I understood you getting angry," he said. "I would have been even angrier if the situation were reversed."

"Everyone pretty much said that I should give you a chance to say what was going on with you and see if it made sense to me. So that's where I am right now. The thing is, I thought we were becoming real friends, and that you liked me. But how could you treat me with such disrespect if you truly liked me?"

"That's the question, isn't it?" Mitch answered quietly, looking down at the rug, clearly feeling shamed. "It doesn't seem as though I could both treat you with such disrespect, as you put it, and like you. You're right. But I really, really like you, Nikki. And if I really care about you, then I have to be out of your life, because of all the things that have happened, because of my family, because of my heritage.

"It wasn't easy to call your mother today, it wasn't easy for me to ask her to have you call me. But I couldn't let you go completely until I had one more talk with you, and saw in your eyes if you despise me."

"I think you can see in my eyes that I don't despise you."

"Yes. I see that. But first, I have to finish telling you all the details. All the terrible details." Mitch stood up and extended his hand to me and helped me to my feet.

I heaved a huge sigh. I was through with terrible troubles, I didn't want any more of it. "There are more terrible details? Where are we going?"

"Next door, to my place."

We went through to the living room where Mom was quietly practicing scales. "I'm going next door, to Mitch's place."

"Don't be long," Mom said.

When we got in the hall, I asked Mitch my other burning questions. "How did you know the emerald ring was mine? How did you know it meant so much to me? How did you return it, when my mother had the locks replaced the next day, and never left the apartment all day?"

"Those are the questions I'm about to answer, Nikki."

We stepped into his apartment. The foyer was very dark, with heavy damask and velvet draperies over the windows. The place looked like it hadn't been touched with a new piece of fabric or stick of furniture in over a hundred years.

"Where's your Mom?" I whispered, and then wondered why I felt compelled to whisper.

"She's taking a nap," Mitch whispered back. "She's been doing a lot of sleeping since the police took my uncle away. She's very depressed. It's a good thing I came back today. It was weak of me to stay away so long, but I had to sort some things out."

"I'm sure your mother understands."

As my eyes adjusted to the darkness, I looked around in awe. "Your apartment is huge! How many bedrooms are there?"

"Five," Mitch answered, taking my hand and leading me down a darkened hall and through a door.

Although the room was very dark, I could make out that there was considerable disarray. Things were piled to the ceiling along all four walls and there was barely room for a small single bed with a tumble of bed sheets on it. It smelled ... not clean.

I pulled back into the doorway. I didn't like the feeling in this horrible, strange, dark place. "Is this your room?"

Mitch hurriedly pushed me back out into the hall. "Heavens! No. I'm sorry, I should have given you some idea of what I'm doing. This is my uncle's room. This room is on the other side of your bedroom. My dear Nikki, this is so difficult for me, but it has to be done. I've just got to get it over with it if I have any hope of being real true friends with you, because you said we had to be perfectly honest, and until I show you this, I'm not perfectly honest. Please help me do it."

Mitch was so obviously miserable that I swallowed my fear and followed him back into his uncle's bedroom. He led me into his uncle's closet. My closet was on the other side of the wall. But on the back wall, instead of a mirror like I had in my closet, I saw a huge sheet of strange-looking dark blue glass. Somehow that shade of blue was familiar, but I couldn't place it.

"What am I looking at?" I asked.

"You're looking at a two-way mirror fixed into a secret door. That's the sheet you put over your mirror."

"It's ... I ... I don't understand. I mean ... I don't understand."

"Let's get out of here." Mitch pulled me out of the closet and out of the nasty, crowded, dark-looking, dark-feeling, dark-smelling room. Wordlessly, he led me across the apartment and down another dark hall, then opened a door to a flood of rosy light. The room was filled with so much light that I blinked and shielded my eyes.

"Sorry." Mitch went to the window and pulled a shade part way so the light was less blinding. I could see Elliott Bay out the window, a stunning view unlike any we had in our apartment.

"Oh! How lovely!" I exclaimed. "What an amazing view."

Mitch turned to me and smiled. The light played around him, and he fairly glowed. He looked like the Angel Gabriel. "It is remarkable." He looked out the window and I went to stand by him.

"Our apartment, being on the end across the whole building has windows on three sides of the building," he said. "Your apartment has east and north exposure, while ours has east, south and west exposure. And to the west, this is the view." There was something regal, proud and sure about him in this moment. Something that came through the ages in his heritage. He didn't seem like a teenager at all, he seemed like a young man who was sorting out his destiny.

I then looked around and saw that I stood in a wonderland of plants. The rosy light poured through a pink, red, yellow and green stained-glass window in the south wall. A narrow antique walnut bed was neatly made and covered with a simple pale green comforter.

Built-in bookshelves of dark, rich walnut filled the wall around the bed, and the shelves were crammed with books. In the corner stood a beautiful antique walnut desk, a couple of walnut chairs, and, under the stained glass window sat an antique love seat. An oriental carpet depicting fantastic animals—unicorns, griffins, and chimeras. covered the hardwood floor.

"So this is your room," I said, in awe.

"Yes," Mitch answered simply.

I could feel him watching me intently as I walked about, quietly studying everything in the room. "It's wonderful," I said. "It's—grown up. My room is like a kid's room, with my posters of rock stars. Here you have a poster of Einstein, and these other guys—I don't even know who they are."

"They're physicists. But I love your room. I love how it shows that you get to be the age you are. I've never been able to just be a kid. There's always this ... responsibility."

He turned from me and looked out the window as if he felt responsible for the very view. "Yes," he went on, "this room reflects what I care about. But I'd like it if I had the opportunity to know enough about contemporary musicians to have a poster of one of them on my wall. Maybe you can help me learn to be younger. I mean, my own age."

"I can try. But," I said, coming back to the situation at hand, "first, please finish telling me about the mirror."

Mitch nodded. He led me to the little love seat, surrounded by gigantic, gorgeous, exotic plants. We sat, and he took my hands in his. He inhaled deeply and held his breath so long, I wondered if he would ever exhale.

Finally, he let his breath out. "Here's the question ... that ... I've been wanting to ask you for a long time. Have you ever ... I mean, has it ever seemed to you that you thought you saw people in your closet mirror?"

I gasped. "Yes! I have. And it has caused me so many problems. It's because of the people in the mirror, when I tried to talk with my mom about it, that made her take me to the counselor. And seeing those people in the mirror made me think that maybe I'm, you know, not quite all right."

A pained expression crossed Mitch's features.

"That has something to do with what you're about to tell me, doesn't it?"

"Yes, Nikki. And here's the story."

I sat perched on the edge of the love seat, in the beautiful glowing rose and yellow light from the stained glass window, while Mitch told me a fantastic story.

"Over a hundred years ago, my great-great-grandfather built this building. The truth of the matter is that my family amassed a great deal of wealth by theft. This theft was considered two things: one, it was an acceptable way of life, and two, it was considered a mark of intelligence, to be 'clever' enough to live off of people who didn't bother to figure out how not to have their possessions stolen.

"It's a mindset that if something could be taken, it needed to be taken. My great-great-grandfather thought it was the height of cleverness to put a two-way mirror in a concealed door into the room that interfaced with his apartment. In other words, your bedroom.

"Then he'd rent that apartment to the wealthiest people he could convince to live there, and go through that door to pilfer things off of them as much as he could get away with. Many an innocent servant and cleaning woman have been dismissed for stealing while they lived with or worked for people who rented that apartment.

"Then my grandfather made a rule that every other tenant in your apartment was not to be plundered. I don't know if he was trying to be more moral or if he feared that one day someone would get caught—as, indeed, has now happened. Anyway, the Rionews have lived there for sixteen years, and as they are the tenants who are not to be robbed, my uncle has become angrier and more frustrated. In particular, because, as you know, they have some very valuable works of art.

"When my mother and I came to live with my uncle, she insisted that he stop all illegal activity. She loved my father deeply, intensely, but she never embraced those 'values' of his family. She insisted that I be raised in an environment of good and moral behavior. Of late, though, my uncle planned to continue as before. He said that I had grown up enough to make my own decisions regarding which path I would follow. Simply put, to him, it's immoral to be moral. He and my mother began to quarrel quite often.

"He loved to perpetuate the rumor that the building was haunted. That rumor started after a fire in eighteen ninety-five, where several people lost their lives in the ballroom that used to be on the floor below us, the sixth floor, which has since been turned into apartments.

"Anyway, getting back to the present, when the Rionews went to Europe my uncle was going to strip the apartment while no one was there, but my mother put her foot down. She reminded him that my father left us well off enough that, living modestly, we don't have to worry about income. But my uncle becomes miserable if he's not stealing.

"My mother argued with him that plundering the Rionews was breaking his father's decree. Just because the Rionews weren't here didn't change the fact that they were the owners of the possessions in the apartment.

When you put that sheet over the mirror, my uncle became furious. I had suspected you could see my him and mother arguing, but my uncle ignored me when I tried to explain that to him.

"The Rionews never used your bedroom, but they had put in new, bright, light fixtures a couple years ago. They packed away the original antique fixtures in the attic, saying we could reinstall them if they moved out, but that they wanted safer and brighter lighting in their home. Anyway, the brighter lights changed the whole effect in the closet. In other words, a person could see this side of the two-way mirror, faintly, if the light was on."

I took in everything Mitch said, more and more clearly understanding what had been going on since I moved into my room. "And so that's how you knew the ring was mine, because you saw me holding it and talking with my grandmother." I looked down, my mind racing, imagining what— or how much—Mitch had seen of me. "So I guess you spied on me too."

"No. I didn't. Like I said, my uncle's room gives me the creeps, so I stay out of it as much as possible.

I just went in there one day to get something, and there you were, sitting on the floor, talking with your grandmother, looking into the emerald.

"I believe in the power of crystals and gemstones. Your relationship with the emerald made a strong impression on me. So when I saw the ring in my uncle's 'goods' as he calls what he steals, I knew that no matter what, I would make sure that your ring, at least, was returned." He paused, then continued softly, "I also made sure that everything else was returned, too. I followed my uncle and secretly called the police with the location of every single thing he fenced."

"You did that? But … that was incredibly brave. If your uncle had seen you or had put it together that you were following him and ratting on him to the police—I hate to think what he might have done."

Mitch grinned a shy, crooked grin and said very softly, "Well, thanks. But I still wish I'd just faced him."

"I think you handled everything amazingly. I can't imagine what I would do if I'd been in your place. Now that I know the whole story, I really admire you!"

I leaned toward him and, under the stained glass window, we shared the most wonderful yellow-red-rosy warm kiss. I relaxed into his arms feeling incredibly relieved. "So, you're telling me there are no ghosts."

"Well, no, I didn't say that," Mitch answered, burying his face in my hair.

Chapter XV
The People in the Mirror

The next Monday, Mitch enrolled in my school, and although I couldn't help feeling uncomfortable about how all the girls stopped in their tracks to look at the "new boy," it was fantastic to see him occasionally between classes.

He was placed in my biology class because the principal said the school could not compromise his science foundation, but the rest of his classes were at the senior level, and he was so happy, it made me happy too.

It was a beautiful sunshiny day, for once, when school let out, and we had a delightful walk home.

"Wait," I said as we passed Mr. Zingas' store, "I want to stop in for a moment and say hi."

"Okay," Mitch said.

The little bell jingled as we walked through the doorway, and Mr. Zingas, alone in the store, looked up at us. "Well, good afternoon Nikki, Mitch. How's it going?"

"Mitch is just coming home from his first day of regular high school, and I feel great!"

"I'm happy for you. Have a seat you two, sit. Just a sec."

Mitch and I sat. Mr. Zingas came over with three fat slices of cheesecake. "Eat, eat." He sat down with us.

"Now then, I have something to say. Once I said an unforgivable thing to Nikki. A prejudiced thing. And I was wrong.

"I must apologize and I have to say that whether a person is a Gypsy or Polish, or Romanian, or American or whatever, it's wrong to say that they are all something bad. Everyone determines for themselves their morals. I was wrong to carry that prejudice, and to feel it against you, my boy, when I could have, and ought to have given you support and understanding for the last five years since you came to live here. I apologize profusely. And I thank you, too."

"Thank me? For what?"

"For teaching an old dog a new trick, that is, not to be judgmental. Your uncle used to come in here and steal right under my eyes. He was, you might be interested to learn, very bad at it. But I was afraid of him, and instead of facing my fear, I let my prejudice include you. Absolutely wrong.

"Both of your mothers came in here together today, giggling like school girls. They were so cute! Then Nikki, your Mom told me about Mitch's bravery and, well, I was hoping he'd come in soon so that I could clear my conscience.

"Even my son, Alex, tried to get me to change my opinion of you, Mitch. He told me a long time ago that you were smart and kind. But I had my own lessons to learn, and you've helped me learn them. More cheesecake?"

By the time we got home my appetite for dinner was ruined. I said good night to Mitch and watched him as he walked down the hall. After all, we were now both high school students, and we had homework to do.

Mom was playing some raucous modern piece of music, the kind that one couldn't tell if she was hitting wrong notes or not, but she appeared to be contented doing it. I grinned and waved as I passed the baby grand on my way to my room. In my closet, the hole of the two-way mirror-door between the two apartments had been sheet-rocked.

I felt a little sorry that there was no longer this doorway to and from Mitch's apartment. I never got to appreciate it while it existed, and now it was gone. My closet was a mess, the workmen would obviously be spending the next day finishing their work because they'd left the huge, heavy, smoky, antique mirror laying on the floor. I stood over the mirror, looking down into it.

No more ghosts, I thought. But even as I watched, the raucous music Mom played faded into the background, and although I could still hear it faintly, the Blue Danube became louder and louder, swelling to the very walls of the closet. There in the mirror materialized a fabulous velvet draped ballroom, sconces of candles on the walls, candles on the tables and on the grand piano, creating an eggshell glow, warm and inviting.

Swirling to the lilting melody danced a roomful of women in billowing gowns and men in formal attire such as I had never seen, from an era long gone, dancing around and around, faster and faster in the smoky glow.

The End

Chapter 1
Not Great News

"I've got great news," Dad announced at dinner.

I felt caution rise up my spine. Dad's "great news" often meant something I would *not* name "great news."

"What's that, dear?" Mom asked. I sensed the same caution from her.

"I have to go back down to Orange County for a few weeks on my job. And now that school's almost out for the summer, we can all be at home for the summer. Of course, we can't stay in our house as it's sublet, but I'll rent a nice little place. Won't that be great! What do you say, Nikki? Summer in Laguna Beach? Great, yes?" He could not have smiled bigger, so pleased with himself.

"Ahh, no, Dad. Not really." How could he not know that I've been looking forward to school getting out with every fiber of my being? Because, one, I'll be able to spend more time with Mitch, and two, my friend Yumi was coming to stay with me for the summer. We've been planning it for *three months*, and I've been babbling on about it, like, *forever*. Where does Dad go when I talk?

Mom glanced at me. There was something in her look that made me even more anxious. "Oh dear," she said.

Dad looked from me to Mom, and from Mom to me. "What am I missing?"

"Quite a lot, Dad. Have you not heard me planning and planning and planning on Yumi coming to stay the summer? … And …."

"Well, yes, I've heard that, yes. But I thought if you were there, that would be altogether better. See?"

"No, Dad. No. The whole point … I mean … hmmmm, if you don't just 'get it' I can't explain it."

Dad shook his head. "I don't get it."

"Well, my dear, there's Mitch," Mom chimed in. "Nikki's looking forward to sharing her life here with her friend, Yumi, and there's Mitch."

"Well, yes," Dad nodded, "Of course, Mitch, I know, there's Mitch. But I thought you'd be so happy to go home for a few weeks. I thought you could stand to be away from Mitch for a while." Dad paused. *"But!"* He lit up like he'd created a brilliant invention. "How about this? Mitch can come down and visit us for a few days, and you could show him Laguna Beach. Now, *there's* a plan!"

I couldn't be mad at him. He was trying. But he still missed the point that my friends and I had been making plans for *weeks*.

"Well," Mom interceded, "that's sweet, dear, although Nikki and her friends have been making a lot of plans for some while. But," and she gave me that apologetic look again, "and I'm sorry, Nikki—I was about to make an announcement at dinner myself. My school called today and begged me to come down and teach in their new summer program for children at risk.

"Well, I jumped at the opportunity! It's an eight-week program, and it's exactly the work that's so meaningful to me." Mom juiced up the apologetic look. "What a strange coincidence, that we both have summer jobs in O.C.!" Mom reached across the table and patted my hand. "I'm sorry, sweetie, to upset your plans, but it looks like we'll all be heading south for the summer."

I looked at Mom, dismayed. "*Ahhhhh ….*" I couldn't add any actual words to my dismay.

"I know, Nikki, it's upsetting, but your dad has a pretty good plan, off the cuff like that. Have Mitch come down and stay with us for a few days."

"But … we were going to go to MoPop and the aquarium, we were going to hang out with Alex, we were going to … oh, so many things!"

I turned my head to look out at the fog hugging the windows like a big soft gray cat, the cozy fog that at first I hated—and had come to love. "Yumi already bought her ticket. She skimped like crazy to get it, and I even gave her some of my allowance. She's coming *day after tomorrow*. Why aren't my plans important? Why can't I just stay here?"

Mom and Dad exchanged a look that said lots, but what, exactly, I could not discern. I plowed on. "First of all, I'm not a little kid anymore, and second, there's Mitch's mom, and there's Homer that I can go to if I need to. And Mr. Zingas, too." I *loved* Alex's dad.

There was that look between Mom and Dad again!

"What I don't get," Dad said, his brow wrinkled, apparently taking in new information, "what I don't get is how all this is going on around me, and I miss it. I thought it was your heart's desire, Nikki, to be home. I thought this would warm the little cockles of your heart."

"Dad, I'm fifteen, almost sixteen, my cockle's desires don't just sit around being the same, day in and day out. Things change. I change. You brought me here, I found friends, and … and I have a special friend, and now … I'm happy here."

"And now you're happy here," he repeated, as if learning a new language.

"I … I suppose I could tell them I'm not available for the summer program after all," Mom said in a small, disappointed voice.

"*No!*" Dad and I practically shouted in unison.

"No, Mom, no. Those kids need you," I insisted, thinking quickly how awful it would be if Mom stayed here, instead of getting involved in a program for at-risk kids. It would likely trigger her occasional depression—and because of me. *Not an option.*

But I wasn't willing to simply give up. "How about a compromise. After Yumi gets here and you two go off to Orange County, let us have a week 'test run.' If things don't go smoothly, then Yumi and I will come down to O.C. at the end of that week."

The eye-language between Mom and Dad again, then Dad nodded. "Okay, my little Pumpkin Patch, we'll give you a few days to prove yourself."

I grinned. When he starts calling me his silly "terms of endearment," I know we're on the right track.

"Daily FaceTime," Mom added. "And *no hesitation* from you if there's any problem."

"A fair contract," I said in my best lawyer-y voice. "Where do I sign?"

"Don't get cocky," Dad advised.

I nodded, trying to put on a sober expression. But my grin threatened to eat my face. What a fantastic outcome—my best friend, Yumi, and me, alone in the gorgeous apartment. Young adults on our own!

And, P.S., Mitch next door.

Nothing could go wrong.

Chapter 11
Best Friends

So two days later we drove to the airport to pick up Yumi and drop off Dad.

It worked out perfectly—we first got Yumi and had a nice little lunch together, then waved good-bye to Dad as he scurried to his flight. Mom would leave the following Monday, taking a Lyft to the airport. I knew it suited her to be sure that Yumi was all settled in. And, well, to simply feel safe to leave the two of us young miscreants to our own devices.

I was *soooo* happy to see Yumi! All we'd shared as best friends since we were little girls came tumbling out the moment we hugged.

"*I missed you!*" she exclaimed in her delicate voice, lightly laced with the hint of Japanese, her first language.

"Me too you! Look at you! More beautiful than ever. How do you do that?"

"Oh!" She tittered softly and looked down shyly. "No, no I'm not. But you are! Something here is very good for you!"

"It's the endless mist. Makes me dewy." I wasn't serious, of course. Just babbling, so delighted to see her.

Dad wrangled us into a restaurant. I was so excited, I could hardly eat, but managed to get down a bowl of soup. The chatter at the table was pleasant but entirely superficial. There was something about Yumi I couldn't put my finger on. She wasn't quite herself.

Was she cautious about being here? Was she, suddenly shy? Had something happened to her that I didn't know about?

As it turned out, I was right on all three points, which would come out over the next few days.

On the drive back to the apartment, Yumi and I sat in the back seat with Mom as our chauffeur. I asked Yumi a raft of questions. She responded with a soft "yes" or "no," or simply shrugged. I had to accept that she just did not want to talk yet. Maybe not in range of Mom's hearing. Maybe not at all. I wasn't sure, but I was sure she was blocking my efforts at a real conversation.

"It's raining," she observed as Mom drove out of the airport and onto the freeway.

"True," I agreed. "That's Seattle. If it's not misting, it's raining. I think I kinda mentioned that." Yeah, like, at first, every day I texted her, "It's misting," "It's raining." Then I got used to it, and stopped with the weather reports.

"I thought," Yumi said, mind-reading, "when you stopped saying every day that it was misting or raining, it had stopped."

Mom and I burst out laughing. "Oh, no! I just got used to it. And I figured, mercifully for you, no doubt, that you didn't need to read that it was doing the same thing that it does every day."

"Oh. *Hmmm*." Yumi fell silent. Did the rain bother her that much? I certainly hoped not.

"Home again," I chirped as Mom drove into our parking structure.

"*Wow!*" Yumi looked up at the gargoyles on the building, "*Protectors!*"

"I guess so," I said, surprised at her observation and even more surprised that she seemed happier to see the gargoyles than to see me. "I never thought of them that way… but of course they're our protectors." We climbed out of the car, gathered Yumi's luggage and backpack from the trunk, then headed for the back entrance to the elevators.

When we stepped inside the back entrance, Homer, the doorman, came up to us while we waited for the elevator. "This must be your charming guest," he tipped his hat ever so slightly.

"Yes, Homer. This is Yumi," Mom said, "Nikki's friend since they were little girls. Yumi, this is Homer, our kindly doorman."

Yumi bowed her head, "Nice to meet you, sir."

"Call me Homer, please."

"All right," Yumi agreed, eyes still averted.

I exchanged a look with Mom over Yumi's head. She was generally quiet and polite, but this was *strange.*

The elevator dinged and the doors slid open. We rode up in silence. When the doors opened on the seventh floor and we stepped into the lovely pale peach light, Yumi sighed audibly.

"What lovely light," she exclaimed.

"I know. I love it," I agreed, relieved to hear a hint of her usual enthusiasm.

We walked down the hall to our apartment, silent footfalls in the dense carpet. Mom unlocked the door and we stepped inside, where the cozy warmth of the apartment embraced us.

"Oh!" Yumi exclaimed, taking in the baby grand, the pale green and apricot facing sofas, the rich walnut of the furniture. *"So beautiful!"*

"I'm glad you like it!" I smiled at her, but she still refused to make eye contact. At a loss, I forged ahead, "Let's get you settled in your room, and then I think Mom made some cookies for us this morning, if I'm not mistaken."

"I did," Mom affirmed, moving toward the piano. "If you don't mind, I'd like to play for a bit while you girls get settled, as I'm soon to leave this glorious piano."

I felt certain that Mom was leaving the two of us alone so I could get to the heart of what was bothering Yumi, and I was grateful for her wordless understanding.

Yumi and I walked down the hall to her guest room. I'd spent a good chunk of my allowance, and hours and hours of my time, putting up posters of her favorite Japanese anime artists that, frankly, I knew very little about. She aspired to become one herself, and if anyone could, it'd be Yumi. Super-talented, she'd already produced a couple of beautiful comics, and even had a small-but-loyal following on the internet.

As the rich tones of Beethoven flowed around us, Yumi took in the posters with a grin. "You put up anime artists just for me in your room?"

"I put up anime artists just for you in your room. This is your very own room. Mine is across the hall," I gestured toward the door.

"*Oh!*" She sounded disappointed.

I had given a lot of thought about sharing my bedroom. Yumi and I had shared my room or her room our whole childhood. But, I thought, if we were living together for several weeks, she'd probably want some space to herself.

But an even more important consideration was my mirror, about which I had two major concerns. The first being, if she saw the people and things in the mirror that I saw on occasion, it would terrify her. The second being, if she never saw anything in the mirror when I did, it would *frighten me!*

"I thought you could use some space to yourself since you're going to be here for a few weeks," I explained. "You like things tidy, and me, well, you know, not so much."

I finally succeeded in making Yumi giggle. "True! Okay, it's good. I love what you've done. Just for me. It's so sweet!" She turned and gave me a hug. "So I guess I get all the drawers and all the closet to myself!"

"Indeed, you do."

I sat on the edge of the bed and watched as she carefully unpacked, deliberately putting each item in a drawer or on hangers in the closet. I knew that I could step into this room at any time, and it would be exactly like this. Neat as a pin.

"Anyway, I'm just across the hall, and my door is always open."

"Yes." Yumi said softly. And again, she seemed to withdraw into some inscrutable place, much more inaccessible to me than my room across the hall.

"How about those cookies?" I asked after her roller board and backpack were neatly stowed in the closet.

"Of course," Yumi nodded, glancing around the room for one last thing daring to be out of place.

"And a tour of the mansion," I suggested.

"I'd like that. It's very impressive, this apartment up here in the clouds." "Very dramatic, isn't it, this weather?"

"Well, I guess so. Lots of shifting energies, yes. I've always felt it."

Yumi nodded. Then, finally, she came over to me, put her arm around my waist and leaned her head against my shoulder. "Thank you for being my friend."

"Oh, Yumi!" I gave her a big hug. "I've really, *really* missed you!" I felt just a bit like crying, overwhelmed with a rush of emotion, glad that she finally warmed up to me, sad that something deeply bothered her.

Arm in arm, we went back to the living room and sat on the sofa, enjoying Mom's amazing playing. *She* would miss it? *I would miss it*, I just realized.

When she finished the piece she turned to us. "Cookies?"

"Of course! And we're going to take a grand tour of the apartment."

"Good idea," Mom agreed. "First let's tour, then we'll hunker down in the kitchen with our warm cookies and tea."

We ambled back down the hall, starting at the far end of the apartment with my room. It was in its usual jumble of a few items of clothing on the bed, and a couple of stacks of books lying about. Not at all bad.

"Goodness, Nikki, your room is as big as an apartment," Yumi exclaimed. "Lots of space to clutter, but it's pretty neat."

"Thanks … probably just a bit in your honor, I pulled it together." As I showed her my giant closet, I flipped on the bright light I'd asked the workers to install when they sheet rocked the wall between my closet and Mitch's uncle's closet. I'd learned that bright light made anything appearing in my mystical mirror invisible.

Then we went into Mom and Dad's room, even bigger than mine, and tastefully luxurious. Of course, it was neat as a pin too, making it seem more likely that Yumi was related to Mom than I.

After appreciating *"The Inner Sanctum"* as I referred to their room, we walked through the living room, and down the hall adjacent to the kitchen, stepping into the beautiful, formal dining room, with a huge vintage walnut table and ten chairs. We almost never ate in here – it was a bit too formal, and the table too-too big for our casual dining.

"Beautiful room!" Yumi exclaimed.

"It is, although we rarely come in here. *Too big!*" Yumi nodded.

Then we stepped back out into the hall and went into the absolutely breath-taking, plant and Art Nouveau statuary-filled, conservatory.

"Oh! *Ohhhhhh!*" Yumi gasped. She studied the spacious room then looked at me incredulously. "You told me you had a room with plants in it. You didn't tell me it was like this – it's an enchanted forest!" She wandered among the exotic plants, eyes wide in wonder.

I trailed along after her, while Mom stood in the doorway. "Well, I didn't say much because, partly, it's hard to describe," I said, "and, partly, I wanted to surprise you when you came. I was sure you'd love it."

Mom joined us as we meandered on the little wandering stone path to the two walls of windows. Looking out, there was nothing to see but the darkening fog.

Yumi turned back to face the room. "I could … I could sleep in here. I would be perfectly happy with a sleeping bag, right here on the floor."

Mom and I exchanged a glance.

"There's a rollaway bed in the hall closet, Yumi. You're welcome to set it up in here if you wish," Mom said. "Honestly, that's a fantastic idea. I've never thought of it."

"Really? I really can do that?"

"If you wish," Mom affirmed. "By the way, Nikki, please do not neglect the plants when I'm gone, you know they need their watering and feeding."

"I'll take care of them, Mom, don't worry."

"That's the one thing the Rionews begged us to do—please take care of the plants."

"The Rionews?" Yumi asked, wandering back among the plants.

"The people we're sub-letting this apartment from," Mom said. "Mr. Rionews works for the same company as Nikki's dad, and he's on a job in England for a year. We were very fortunate to be able to lease this beautiful place for the time being."

"You certainly are! Please let me help Nikki take care of the plants."

"Of course, Yumi, if you'd like."

"I would very much like."

Finally, we made our way back to the kitchen. Mom set out the cookies and put water on for tea, and soon we were munching on delicious fresh cookies filled to the brim with chocolate chips and sipping tea, while Mom read aloud the four pages of "Plant Care" the Rionews had left for us.

I felt myself experiencing an emotion I didn't like. I'd gone from thinking it best if Yumi and I each had a bedroom across the hall from one another, to being strangely disappointed that she wanted to sleep in the plant room, at the *complete opposite end of the apartment*.

You are very silly, I said silently to myself, watching Yumi's enthusiasm as she and Mom pored over the plant document. But my self-reprimand did not dissuade the niggling emotion one little bit.

Thank you ....

For reading Nikki's story, ***The People in the Mirror***.

Nikki has continuing adventures in **Millie in the Mirror**, where she, Mitch, and her close friends, Yumi and Alex continue to explore Seattle's mysterious *Underground City*.

And the paranormal fun and romance advance to a whole new level in **The Angel in the Mirror**.

Is there a story you'd like to read about Nikki's adventures? We'd love to hear about it!

If you've enjoyed Nikki's story perhaps you'd write a review as readers are interested in what other readers have to say about a story. And we love to know what our readers have to say!

Until Next Time,

Thea Thomas

&

Blythe Ayne

www.BlytheAyne.com

About Thea ....

I live in the greater Portland, Oregon area. I love the Great Northwest where the rainy weather, lush green territory, waterfalls, mountains, charming neighborhoods, the Pacific ocean nearby, and a strong writing community—all contributing to making my writing life a dream come true.

You can write to me at:

Thea@EmersonandTilman.com

Have a Happy Day!
Thea

About Blythe ....

I live in a forest with a few domestic and numerous wild creatures, where I create an ever-growing inventory of books and short stories, with a bit of wood carving when I need a change of pace.

All the creatures in my forest and I are glad you "stopped by." If you enjoyed *The People in the Mirror*, I hope you'll share it with others.

If you'd like to write me, I'd be happy to hear from you!

Blythe@BlytheAyne.com

www.BlytheAyne.com

'Til We Meet Again!
Blythe